A

FISTFUL OF HOLLERS

OR HOW THE WEST GOT SILLY

Edited by
Crystalwizard, Lyn Perry, and Y.B. Cats

Published by CyberAliens Press

A Fistful of Hollers: Stories & Poems on How the West Got Silly
Compiled and edited by Crystalwizard, Lyn Perry, and Y.B. Cats
Compilation copyright © 2010 Cyberwizard Productions
Each work copyright © 2010 by the Individual Author
Cover design and interior illustrations Copyright © 2010 by Richard Svensson
ISBN: 978-1-936021-24-6
Library of Congress Control Number: 2010903916

Published by CyberAliens Press, an imprint of Cyberwizard Productions
1205 N. Saginaw Blvd, #D, PMB 224
Saginaw, Texas 76179

www.cyberwizardproductions.com

A FISTFUL OF HOLLERS

BILLY STEADMAN, THE DRAGON AND THE FISHING HOLE

Dal Jeanis

A few months after his wedding, Billy Steadman felt the urge to go fishing. Billy considered that urge—rolled it around in his head pretty much the way his tongue couldn't help exploring that newly missing tooth, the one he lost on his wedding night.

It wasn't that Billy liked fishing; it was that being around dragons made him nervous. No, that wasn't it either. A man could get used to having a dragon around, even a pregnant dragon, as long as it kept eating iron and pooping gold. A man could get used to having a great big spread of land centered on the dragon's abandoned iron mine, with a thousand head of cattle and a ten room main house built (metal-free) with that gold. A man could get used to all that.

But there were other things.

The first thing that was hard to get used to was his new wife fluttering about that ten-room house, putting up curtains and taking them down, dying them different colors, replacing them with different frilly things, and shooing him out of the way whenever he managed to sit down for a minute and a half. Or worse, making him hold up things or move furniture or calling him into the bedroom and asking what she looked like in a different dress. He shuddered; both experience and his missing tooth told him there was no right answer to that question.

The second thing that was hard to get used to was the way people treated him now. Cash money had crowned him 'Mister Steadman', like he was suddenly his own grandfather or some such nonsense. And the way people kept using highfaluting words and fixing on things that made no blamed sense. Sure, Miss Daisy —er, Missus Daisy Steadman, his bride — seemed to expect a lot of her new husband, but darned if he could puzzle out why they called her "expectant" rather than "bossy." And the guys down at the saloon — yes, he had managed to sidetrack enough gold to see that a saloon got built in downtown Bent Axle — those guys suddenly seemed oddly interested in whether Billy could count backwards. Billy had never had a head for figuring, but he'd have thought that people drinking his whiskey at quite affordable prices would have had other things on their mind than mathematics.

At least when he'd been poor, Billy had known what they were laughing at.

So, hiding out in the tiny attic space that Daisy hadn't managed to choke yet with doilies and froofraws, Billy commenced to begin to start to consider to decide to… darn it, he was going fishing.

"Billy?" Distant.

But first, he had to get out the front door. The moccasins would make that easier.

"Billy Steadman?" Distant, but getting nearer. That sweet Southern voice still held a lilt, so perhaps he wasn't in trouble yet. The boys down at the saloon said that dealing with women was an art. Well, Billy Steadman didn't think of himself as no artist — at least not unless some fool invented a kind of art where you just splattered color every which way and called it a painting. Billy hadn't a clue, but at least he wasn't fooling himself. And once that woman got herself into a spitfire frenzy, there weren't nothing for it except to hang on to your hat and wait it out while the paint went flying.

With a last, yearning glance back up at the attic, he stowed the ladder and made for the hall.

"Billy!"

Too late.

Good God, he wanted to be fishing. Anywhere but here. Just up at the pond would be fine.

"Yes, dear?" It just sort of slipped out while he was thinking about other things. Unintentional.

That pond down above the mine tailings wasn't intentional, either, no more than half the things that people do in a hurry. If the miners had thought about it, they probably wouldn't have dropped the tailings right there, but they also might not have cared one way or the other; the marginally useful presence of the pond for washing up once or twice a week would have been just about balanced by having to ride an extra half mile every time you went to town. But, they didn't think about it much if at all; it just sort of happened.

Just like his marriage.

2

"Billy Steadman, we need to have a talk."

A talk. Billy felt the start of the inexorable slide into the mud pit of a woman's conversation. Put Daisy in a room, and that room would fill up with her talking. Unless she was furious, in which case the room would fill up with her silence.

Just like the pond, really. If you scooped out a hole in the ground in this part of Texas, it would fill with water during the rainy season, then dry out during the dry season. If you scooped it deep enough, then it would fill up during the rainy years and empty out during the drought years. And if you found a place that was naturally deep, then all you had to do was dam the lower end, and you had yourself a lake, instant and permanent. Well, those mine tailings had accidentally made a natural dam, and the water the miners were diverting from the nearby Gribble River for use in the mine had just sort of collected into a small and murky lake.

"Now, Billy, I sent you down to town for pickles, and what did you bring me?"

Billy shook himself and loosened his collar, wondering where this was going. "Pickles."

"In what?"

She stepped close, and the smell of lavender encircled him. The sweetness in her voice was deceptive, but it pulled him in nonetheless. Like she was the fisherman, and he was a fish... "In a barrel."

The fish stuck in that lake had apparently gotten there by accident of a river flood or by taking a wrong dodge through the mining operation. There weren't many, and they didn't seem happy for being there. The last one Billy caught was a year back, after a half day of fishing in the reddish waters. The captured fish didn't fight much — it just looked at Billy with these accusing, staring yellow eyes, like it was all his fault somehow. After pondering on that possibility for a while, Billy had shrugged, and cooked and ate that fish anyway, a taste just like eating nails, only slightly less crunchy.

"And what was around the barrel?" The word "around" did a little vocal dance as Daisy's arms slipped around him and fastened. Daisy looked up at him with a private intensity, and he couldn't help feeling her slender dance hall body through her starched dress. Billy fought against the confusion.

Fishing. Think about fishing.

"A rope?"

Billy didn't figure he ever wanted to eat another fish from that pond. It didn't matter, though. Fishing wasn't about eating. There was something pure about fishing, that allowed a man to clear his head. It might be the calm light reflecting off the water. It might be the feel of the rod in his hand.

"Inside the rope."

More likely it was the fact that there wouldn't be no women there chattering up a storm, filling his belly with unsettled feelings and his head with things that made no sense whatsoever.

"Are you listening to me, Billy Steadman?"

"Yes, Ma'am."

Course, that might not just be Daisy. Billy's daddy had always said that if you could round up all the stray thoughts in Billy's head, you'd have yourself the strangest trail drive in history.

"What was around the barrel?"

"Nothing, Daisy. It was a plain barrel, with pickles, oak planks, and those circle thingies that hold the barrel together.?

"Which were made of...?"

In a flash, Billy knew where this was going. Those circles were made of metal. Which meant that the dragon had...

"So, you need another barrel of pickles?" He felt a surge of hope. If he worked this out right, he could have a man from town deliver the pickles and be off to go fishing without any fuss at all.

Her sigh could have been any number of things. "Yes, Billy."

"I'll get right on that." This could work out right nice.

"Then get right back after, y'hear?"

Billy headed out back to the two-seat outhouse for the necessary preliminaries before he could head to town. Like everything else on the spread, the outhouse was built with pegs and leather straps and other carpentry things that only people who loved wood would understand. The only protection from that dragon that Daisy called "Goose" was making sure there wasn't any metal other than gold anywhere within smelling range of the mine. And Goose's smelling range was apparently several miles.

Daisy's was a mite less than that.

Nevertheless, Daisy had recently taken an intense dislike to Billy Steadman's long-suffering hat. Billy had kept that hat through the bad times and the worse times, and it had survived through shootings and dunkings and droppings in fluid mixtures that by rights should have left it able to walk around on its own. In that first meet-up with Goose, the hat had ended up squashed in horse guts, which really weren't all that bad as stink goes. It had cleaned up pretty well afterwards, and the incident with the coyote vomit didn't do much harm, neither.

In any case, Daisy wouldn't allow his lucky hat into the house. To keep peace with his bride, he kept it in the outhouse, where it only seemed part of the natural fragrance of the place.

But, fishing, he could wear his hat.

He stood on the outhouse seat, carefully straddling the holes, then reached up into the roof notch where his hat was stored.

A pain stabbed his finger. A screeching rat leaped onto his face, scratched a line down across his neck and skittered into the back of his shirt. Billy jumped, his hands heading for his shirt and his head bumping on the roof. Then he came down, his foot landing in the hole. That foot kept going, and the other stopped flat, so Billy swung over and slammed against the side of the outhouse. As he bounced the other direction, his mind had a split second to flash, *"Thank God, it held!"* in badly spelled words across Billy's mental slate-board.

Then the rat ran around in front of him and scrabbled at his chest, ripping a mouthful of chest hair before it headed south. Billy screamed and kicked, and his free foot snapped a leather strap.

The outhouse went over and flew to pieces. The top chunk literally flew, wobbling off like a drunken bird, and then, apparently thinking better of the matter, flipping itself over to land slap-dab on a nearby bush. The sides fell to pieces, except the parts still lashed together by leather straps. *Those* parts whipped out, then accordioned back, and slammed down to cover the otherwise soft ground that Billy's head was heading for. The base, with its two-holed seat and solid carpentry, remained where it had started, the exception being that now it stood proudly in the open, right out in front of God and everybody.

Billy, by some happy miracle, had managed to yank his trapped leg out of that hole rather than having it snapped off at the ankle. That would have been it, under normal circumstances.

However, Daisy had wanted that house built where it wouldn't have to look at the scabbed-over land around that mine, or the auburn-colored pond that had built up behind those tailings. Which meant that the house had to be the other side of a hill from them. Which meant that outhouse was also on a hill. Which meant that Billy was going for a ride.

Now, Billy had found from sad experience that a ride on a broken outhouse worked out best if you kept your butt centered on a big solid slat, your feet in front of you, and a pair of heavy boots ready to kick out at any snake or critter that happened to be unlucky enough to wander itself onto the slope below you. The Law of Averages has it that occasionally, just kind of at random, it truly does work out that way. On the other hand, the Law of Steadman has it that this time, as usual, he was face down, crosswise, on a mixed heap of slats, wearing moccasins, and with a rat inside his britches.

And that was how the ride started.

During the slide down, Billy was too busy to notice the details about the rattlesnake or the mesquite or the cactuses. It was barely within his awareness that it happened to be three armadillos, one large and two small, who rode with him during the second half of the trip, and whose rolled-up bodies shot off down slope when Billy came violently to rest against that last clump of mesquite. The main thing in Billy's brain during that trip was a great thumping and crashing, and how much he'd rather be fishing.

Then a big *OWWW*.

Billy lay for a moment, feeling for anything broken. Nothing but his dignity, and he really hadn't been able to feel that in a long, long time.

He looked up at the sky, past the mesquite bush to the blue. Something about this one mesquite was familiar. He'd been here before. Oh, yes. The one with the ant hill.

Billy Steadman jumped up and flailed his limbs to brush and kick ants off his extremities. Not much in the way of itching, and somewhere in the ride that rat had disappeared, a small blessing that he was willing to accept gratefully.

He should have known better. In actuality, the rat had gone nowhere. It was just so terrified by that careening descent that it had become merely a stiff fuzzy spot on the loose tail of Billy's shirt. The petrified rat didn't even move during the majority of Billy's trudge back up the hill. It just panted, wide-eyed, and waited for the world to stop spinning and shaking. Eventually the familiar smell of the outhouse worked its way through its rat-mind, and it remembered what it had been doing. Fear was replaced by indignation, indignation by outrage—and outrage began looking for a target.

So, just as Billy leaned down to pick up the battered roof, the rat resumed its assault with a sneak attack on his backside. A line of fire spread from his butt up and across Billy's back, and Billy flipped over and rolled several times before he came up against the outhouse base and realized there wasn't any campfire for him to have gotten too close to.

Swearing, Billy ripped his shirt open and groped for the rat. It leaped out and dropped through one of the potty holes into the darkness of the pit. He propped himself up for a moment, then fell back, panting.

He was going to kill that rat.

He lay, looking up at the blue sky, and puffy white clouds flowing in clumps from the south. He breathed in the smell of crushed grass and splintered pine.

He let the breath out.

Yep, he would kill that rat. He'd do that tomorrow, after he went fishing.

Billy stood, gathered together his shirt, and checked himself for damage. He dabbed a handkerchief on his scratches and stepped back over to where the roof had fallen. Reaching into the remains of the roof, he retrieved his long-suffering hat. Inside the hat were straw, rat droppings, and five baby rats, their eyes still closed.

Billy looked over at the potty hole, and considered for a moment. Their mommy had gone that way; he could drop them into that hole in clear conscience. He surely could. Yep, he surely could...

Billy gazed at the hole for a long moment. Finally, Billy folded the straw and the rat-pups into his bloody handkerchief and set them into the shade beside the destroyed outhouse. Then

7

he turned towards the corral.

"Billy?"

He froze. "Yes, Daisy?"

"You don't mean to leave the 'necessary' in that condition... do you, Billy?"

Billy's glance lingered on the corral, then moved to the pieces scattered down slope, then he turned back to the house, seventy feet away, where Daisy stood with her hands resting easily on her hips. She wasn't even raising her voice, but he heard every syllable.

"No Ma'am."

Daisy nodded, and disappeared into the house.

Fixing the outhouse—collecting it, lashing it together and propping it up as best he could—took three hours, and it still looked haggard for its experience. It put Billy in mind of that coyote that had gotten into the tequila, except that the outhouse didn't cringe whenever he made a noise. The john would hold, barely, until he could get a real carpenter to have a look.

And anyway, he was getting hungry.

With that special sense of women, Daisy anticipated Billy's attempt to come inside for a late lunch and she stood up at the house, blockading the doorway with arms crossed. When Billy got halfway to her, just about thirty feet away, she moved one dainty hand up to hold her nose. The other pointed toward the wash bucket she had left nearly at his feet. He got the message.

Washed and changed, and fed with Daisy's latest creation — possum and pickle pie — Billy finally escaped to the corral, where he put his all-leather tack onto his roan stallion. The horse looked at him, glanced to his hat, and nickered. Snickered, more like. He reached to touch his gun in warning, then remembered he couldn't keep one, not with that dragon slurping up anything iron or lead in the neighborhood. Too bad you couldn't make guns out of clay or something light and moldable. Maybe in a bright color, too, so you wouldn't forget where you left it. No, that didn't make no sense.

The roan snickered again. Billy took a few small gold ingots from the travel pile and loaded them into the saddlebags. He might as well carry them down to the bank if he was going there anyway. He bent down to check the hard leather bags tied over the roan's feet, then mounted and started for town. It was a glorious day for fishing.

He passed the lake, letting his gaze slide lovingly along the banks and pick out likely spots. He promised himself he'd be back soon to take advantage of the shade of that tree, the one right there, where he could drop in his line and lay back on the summer-bronzed grass—even if it was spring.

On the other side of the pond, he pulled up on the rise, sat the horse there for a minute or two just pretend-fishing: dropping a mental line all the way past the dark dam of mine tailings to the russet water beyond; smelling the water and fish poop and plant smells; listening to the wind and the birds.

Finally, Billy closed his eyes against the glorious auburn sight, and turned his roan toward the town of Bent Axle, to order another — non-metal this time — barrel of pickles.

Bent Axle was fair sized as places went in this part of Texas. There were probably three hundred residents in the town itself, and perhaps that many again of the local farmers who kept their money in A.J. Wylie's bank down there. It was the only bank in Texas with a wooden vault and three tons of gold.

It wasn't that they needed that much gold in town. It was just that gold never seemed to leave as fast as it came in. You couldn't just put the stuff into a shipping wagon—Goose was drawn to large concentrations of metal, even gold, and she only got around to ignoring the gold after she tore everything else apart checking for stray nails and horseshoes.

Billy knew, from his short stint as Sherriff and his large account with Wylie, that they used fast couriers, no more than three horses at a time, to carry sixty thousand dollars of gold twice a day to a rendezvous with a Wells Fargo strongbox. They couldn't outrun the dragon, but the couriers were timed to coincide with regular shipments of pig-iron that Wylie had arranged to be left north of Goose's mine. Wylie was building up an excellent balance in banks as far away as Abilene and Kansas City. But it didn't make a dent in the pileup of gold, not with having to be subtle and all.

Even the inevitable bank robbers—when they came to town, broke into the vault and tried to carry off a few hundred pounds—just seemed to be calling attention to themselves. Somewhere out along their escape route they would hear the beating of wings, and later the locals would find them, gunless, among the remains of their horses, but generally alive and babbling like complete idiots. And with a pile of gold larger than the one they tried to steal. The locals would sigh, hand the robbers some moccasins, and transport the whole mess home to the all-wooden jail in town.

Billy smiled. Apparently once Daisy had taught the dragon that people shoes could come off, Goose had become quite picky about not getting flesh or blood mixed up with the good stuff—the little iron and copper tidbits that held the shoe leather together. Billy didn't know how long dragon pregnancies lasted, but whenever the end was, he was looking forward to being able to wear something other than moccasins again. And to own a gun.

But in the meantime, Bent Axle had managed to pile up a couple million dollars worth of gold, and it showed no sign of slowing down. Some of the locals were talking of renaming the town 'Steadmanville', or some such. Billy shook his head, and rode into town to Dutch Sampson's General Store.

Billy would have been hard pressed to explain Dutch Sampson to anyone who hadn't lived here. All these strangers who wandered through town to take a shot at what they were now calling 'Steadman's Gold Rush' either laughed at the man or just plain stared. But then, if they laughed, it was only once. People around here liked Dutch.

The men, they liked Dutch because he had the best jokes and the best right hook and the best advice you could ever hope to hear on just about any subject. He got along well with his wife and kids, treated everyone with respect and kept folks pretty well straight down the middle, no matter what he chose to wear.

The women, they liked Dutch because he had the best fabrics and the best taste and the best dress patterns in the northern half of the state. And he could tell a woman exactly how to alter a pattern to make the most of her natural attributes. Dutch could do this, and do it well, because he had so much experience altering those patterns for himself.

Today, Dutch was wearing a blue gingham dress with

a floppy blue hat, honoring the spring. He listened to Billy's recount of the day, including the ride on the outhouse, and then took the order for the pickles, to be delivered when available. Billy also took delivery of a new wooden pole, hemp string from Gribble Gulch, and half a dozen hooks made of carved bone.

He paid with an ingot, with the remainder credited to his account. Billy then headed down to the assayer's office, where he found Old Elmer in talks with that British fellow, Mr. Gerald Scrimshaw. Scrimshaw was the British gentleman who had identified Daisy's one-horned dragon as the first known example of a pregnant *draconis verdigrii*, which apparently explained all the strange doings with the metal and the poop. Or it *would* explain it for the next time, once Scrimshaw finished writing up all his findings for the Academy of Royal whatsis in England.

Elmer was the town assayer and undertaker, which together had been a part-time job before the arrival of Goose. Now he had a number of assistant assayers with wooden shovels.

Billy told them the story of the outhouse, complete with the details of the ride down the hill.

Scrimshaw frowned. "A troublesome allegory."

Billy wondered if that was some sort of sports term, like that polo thing that Scrimshaw had mentioned once. Billy had heard of bobsledding, where people rode things down hill on purpose. Seemed like a lot of damn foolishness, but so did much of life. He looked back up into Scrimshaw's face.

Scrimshaw considered Billy for a moment, then gingerly asked, "Have you determined the identity of the snake?"

He hadn't actually got more than a glimpse before it dived back off the slats. "Just some rattler, I figure. It don't matter none."

"That's quite magnanimous of you."

Billy squinted at the Englishman's face, and finally decided that was a compliment. "Thank you kindly."

Billy was heading for his horse when he heard a great thump-bumping out behind the buildings. What was that fool dragon up to now?

He drew in his breath then let it out. Fishing. Think of fishing. Then he walked into the alley to investigate. It turned out that for once the rug-beating noise was actually a woman beating a rug.

11

Susan Carter was younger than Billy Steadman, with a clean, unlined face and hands still soft, at least on the backsides. She wore a periwinkle work dress and blue bonnet, and rhythmically thrashed the rug with a wooden beater, muttering under her breath. Billy stopped and smiled, then cleared his throat.

Susan turned and jumped.

"Oh, Billy." Her face melted through a couple of different expressions he couldn't read, then smoothed to one he knew well, a tentative smile. He wasn't in trouble yet. Which was a good thing, since Susan was one of the excitable women that cried at weddings and ran off at odd times.

"How-do, Susan."

Susan's eyes sought the ground. Her hands fluttered a bit, then she started fanning herself, perhaps just to keep away the smell of Billy's hat. "I heard, Billy. It was a terrible thing to hear."

"I didn't think it was all that bad."

She searched his face, first with doubt then with a kind of wonder. "You are such a forgiving man."

Forgiving? Not like those rat pups had done anything other than sleep in the hat. "Well, it don't make much sense to hold babies accountable for what their mommas do."

Something in Susan's carriage changed, like she grew an inch and her shoulders squared off. Billy couldn't help but notice that Susan was full a woman. "It's so much less than you deserve. How you can even attempt to keep things together after..."

While her voice trailed off, Billy considered the outhouse. It was pretty hard for him to put back together himself, and he did have the money. "Well, I am kind of getting used to having things like that done for me."

A sharp look passed across Susan's face, and her breath came out in a huff. "You are a peculiar man, Billy Steadman."

He looked after her as she closed the back door to the store, leaving Billy and the rug standing bewildered. After a decent interval had passed, Billy decided to head home to his fishing hole.

It was just a little bit along that he would come over a rise and see the lake. He might pause again to sit the roan up there for a minute or two just pretend-fishing. That might be nice. Yes, that might hold him until he could get on around to his fishing spot and bait a hook. He'd just sit on that rise and listen to the chirping of baby birds and smell the lake. In fact, the smell of the lake was already reaching him, a bit more marshy than usual, with wet vegetation and rot rather than just the usual rusty water and fish poop smell.

He crested the rise, and his eyes sought the auburn glory of the lake.

They found, instead, a pattern of green and mirrors and red-brown muck, spread across hundreds of acres of ground. And there, where the dam of mine tailings should be, was that dragon Goose, scrabbling like a dog in a dump.

He really would have to kill that dragon someday. He certainly would.

Billy closed his eyes against the sight; let a tear drip on down his face. Even the roan was silent and after a puff of swampy wind, the birds held their breath as well.

Then, on its own, the roan began to move. The horse picked its way along the washed out road as Billy sobbed, and the sun started to take on a color like the water rusted by those mine tailings. It was just too damn much.

Billy closed his eyes and felt the swaying, swaying, as the horse turned off the road and up and over a small hill away from Daisy's ten room house, walking off into the scrubby woods that led to the neighbor's spread. Billy gave the roan its head, since there wasn't a damn thing in life that would ever work out the way that Billy wanted it.

There wasn't a good thing in life that couldn't just rust away.

Fifteen or twenty minutes later, Billy realized he was tensing where the mother rat had scratched him so much earlier today. He tried to let the tension go, but the squeaking was setting him on edge. Squeaking and rumbling.

Billy opened his eyes. The roan was approaching the stock pond on his neighbor's property, where a small wooden windmill pumped water through clay pipes to the pond. The roan walked in up to its knees and drank, then blew.

The water was clear and clean.

The sun was setting when Billy dismounted the roan and tied him to a tree by the pond. Feeling a profound sense of peace, he took a deep breath and tossed out his line.

The hook dropped into the stock pond, sending ripples cascading out to reflect off the edges and mirror back to meet in the center.

Billy let out his breath in a deep, deep sigh.

Then his eyes widened in surprise, and he swore.

"By God! Daisy's pregnant!"

TALL TALE
Will Morton

The range I was ridin' was still,
An' I come upon ol' Pecos Bill.
We chewed his tobaccer,
An' spit 'crost an acre,
Th' Grand Canyon we come nigh to fill.

WINDY HORSES
Melanie Pearce

The wagon sped across the plain
As fast as it could go.
The Indian drums echoed all around
From the frightening Arapaho.

Jeb and Charlie saw the natives
Watching from a cliff.
Charlie held on to his hat
And Jeb held down his quiff.

"We need to think of something quick."
Said Charlie, "Something drastic."
Then Charlie looked back in the wagon

And had an idea dang fantastic.

Jeb saw the Indians coming fast
A hollerin' and a whoopin'.
Charlie yelled "Find a place to stop!"
And picked up a silver baked-bean tin.

Charlie opened those baked-bean cans,
He shouted, "get yer boots off Jeb."
Jeb looked at him kinda funny
Until an arrow whizzed past his head.

"Come on Jeb, fill your boots
With these tasty old baked-beans.
"We'll outrun those pesky Indians,
We'll feed them to the team."

So they quickly made four nosebags
And the horses loved them beans,
But an Indian went riding by
And they knew they had been seen.

The Indian blew a horn and signalled
Back to the clan with glee.
The Chief said, "Let's scalp those wily white men
And get back home for tea."

Then suddenly the horses began to stomp
And get real restless,
And it started small and slowly
But the atmosphere became poisonous.

Jeb and Charlie covered their nose and mouth
But their poor blue eyes watered
As beany gases began to work their way
To the nags hindquarters.

Jeb shouted "Go" and the horses
Carried on across the plain.
The Arapaho were catching up
With Jeb and Charlie's wagon again.

Suddenly the mighty Chief
He pulled alongside Jeb.

He raised his bow and arrow
And aimed right for his head.

Jeb prayed to God he'd live to see
His pretty sweetheart Jean.
Then the horses let off a noxious gas
And the air around turned green.

The Chief turned a funny shade of green too
And nearly lost his lunch
Jeb took the chance, he raised his fist
And gave his hardest punch.

The Chief he fell down from his horse
And the wagon sped away.
He picked up a silver baked-bean can
And he was heard to say.

"Let the stinky white men go
I need to get a bath.
They'll soon come to regret the day
They left a baked-bean can in my path."

The horses made it back to Dodge
Within no time at all.
Although it took some time
Before their bums began to cool.

It was a stinky day in Dodge
But Jeb and Charlie didn't mind
They'd outwitted the Indians
And left them far behind.

The Indian Chief didn't feel like
Chasing wagons for a while
Although it's heard his experiments
With beans were rather wild.

Jeb married his sweetheart Jean
And they lived happy ever after.
They had 2 kids, a dog, a cat,
And their lives were filled with laughter.

Charlie became famous

Advertising baked-beans with his team.
There was never a stinkier heroic deed
In history to be seen.

Gas Warfare
Gary R. Hoffman

"Well, Matthew, what are you gonna do about this?"

"Don't see that I have a choice, Doc. I gotta face this bunch and see they don't try and take over Plymouth."

"But Marshall Dill," Chico said, "these are supposed to be some of the meanest hombres this side of the Pecos."

Matt plunked his shot glass on the bar. "Chico, first of all, the Pecos is a long way from here. Second, it runs north and south. We're on neither side of it. Comin' from where you do, I'd thought you'd figure that out."

"Never understood why my mama named me Chico," he said. "Our family sure ain't Mexican."

Just then, Miss Kitten, the owner of the Short Stick Bar, came strutting down the steps. "From my window, saw four men ride into town, Matt. Might be the guys you're waiting for."

"Miss Kitten," Chico said, "I got a question for you. All the years I've known you, you come waltzing down here wearing them low-cut dresses with half your bosoms hanging out and yet you say there is nothin' fishy going on here. Looks to me like you're advertisin'."

Doc took off his hat and slapped Chico on the shoulder with it. "Why that's the dangest fool question I ever heard, and I thought I had heard 'em all from you."

"Well, I just thought a feller's got the right to know since we spend so much time here."

"Stupidest thing I ever heard," Doc said.

Miss Kitten tweaked Chico under the chin. "You'll never know, darlin'."

The sound hoof beats was heard coming from somewhere

17

outside. "Guess I better get out there," Matt said.

"I'll go up on the roof and be a look-out," Chico said.

Miss Kitten stepped in front of him. "Be careful out there, Matt. I need you back here tonight." She kissed him on the cheek.

"Gotta get them out of Plymouth," he said and walked through the swinging doors of the Short Stick. He went to the middle of the street just as the four men rounded the corner, adjusted his gun belt, and shook his hand to get it loose. He then raised his other hand in the air to stop the men.

"Hey, a traffic cop all the way out here," one of them said.

"Joe, that was totally uncalled for," Hoss said.

"I'm Marshall Dill. Identify yourselves."

The older of the men spoke up. "I'm Ben Cartwrong, and these are my sons, Joe, Hoss, and Adam."

"What's your business in Plymouth?"

"We been out looking for strays. Thought we'd stop here for the night."

"Where's your spread, mister?" Dill asked.

"Virgin City."

"Virgin City? I heard tell that name really doesn't apply anymore."

Ben squirmed on his saddle. "Well, Joe does get a little crazy when he goes into town…sometimes."

"Another thing. You boys are a long ways from home. Virgin City is in Nevada. This is Kansas."

"Well, we got the biggest ranch anywheres around there and the biggest and best cattle. Sometimes they roam mighty far."

"According to my calculations and based on the speed they can travel, we should be just a few hours behind them," Adam said.

Ben shook his head and whispered to Matt. "College education. Real smart-ass!"

"I think I remember hearin' about you," Hoss said. "Weren't you called Dill Pickle in high school?"

Matt blushed and heard Miss Kitten laugh from somewhere behind a window of the Short Stick. She had poked Doc in the back and laughed again. "He was called that because

18

of what his… never mind."

"Got another question," Matt said. "On your way over here did you happen to run into any other gangs of men headed in this direction?"

"Only saw two other men on horses. One was wearing a mask and riding a huge white stallion. He had his faithful Indian companion with him," Ben answered.

"How do you know the Indian was his faithful companion?" Matt asked.

Adam shook his head. "He told us so."

"And you believed a masked man?"

"The dude was wearing silver bullets on his gun belt. You don't question someone like that," Hoss said.

"See anyone else?" Matt asked.

"Nobody on horses, but we saw several guys walking."

"Walking? Across Kansas? They'll be bored to death by the time they get here. How many of them were there?"

Ben looked at his sons for agreement. "Oh, thirty or forty. We didn't really stop to count them. We smelled them from quite a ways off, so we didn't get too close."

"I think they may have been members of the Hole-in-the-Wall Gang," Adam said.

"And why's that?" Matt asked.

"From my research," Adam continued, "Moondance's girlfriend, Molly Clapsaddle, wouldn't let them use the bathtub because there was a hole in the wall where the tub was located, and they all slopped water out and onto her kitchen floor. Hence, the Hole-in-the-Wall Gang."

"Hum," said Matt. "So that's why they smell like they do."

"Precisely!" Adam said and smiled. Ben shook his head. Joe eyed a busty young woman walking along the boardwalk. Hoss rose up slightly on his saddle, tilted to the side, and cut the cheese. Fortunately, the wind was blowing away from Matt.

Chico yelled from the rooftop. "A bunch of guys was walkin' into town, Mr. Dill, but they got a whiff of that one Hoss cut, and they turned around and left. Must'a been some smell."

Ben shook his head. "That's not hard to believe. I've been smellin' those things for years. Gassiest kid I ever met."

"Maybe we could bottle up somethin' like that," Matt

said. "We could call it nerve gas. Nobody else would have the nerve to use it."

"Maybe in the future," Adam said. "Maybe in the future."

Wrong-way Cowboy
Will Morton

Drivin' longhorns to ol' Abilene,
The boss he was mule-headed mean.
But his compass was broke,
An' he 'bout like to choke
When we halted outside New Orleans.

Circumstantial Evidence
Gary Every

Everyone in the courtroom was convinced beyond the shadow of a doubt that Feldspar Quartz was guilty of thievery like the charges read. The trial was mostly a formality until the gathered crowd could view the afternoon's entertainment. It was anticipated that the high point of the day's festivities would be the hanging of Feldspar Quartz. Some people had forsaken the trial and had already gotten the good seats in front of the hanging tree. The joke around town was that one did not want to be downwind of Feldspar when he swinging from the noose. The cranky old prospector was not known for bathing regularly.

Even Feldspar Quartz's lawyer thought he was guilty but still that would not prevent him from the best legal defense he could offer. Lance Sterling had ignored the signs outside of town which read: "No stray dogs, Indians, or lawyers allowed", walked right in, and set up a law office across the street from the busiest saloon in town. Wherever there was that much alcohol, prostitution, and gambling, a lawyer was sure to flourish. Lance was a pretty smart guy, Harvard educated and all, what he was doing out west was anybody's guess, but the rumors said it had something to do with a Senator's wife. Business in the little mining town of Butte, Montana had been booming for Lance Sterling ever since he had set up shop but to tell the truth this

20

was the first time he had ever brought a case to trial and he knew that it was important that he make a good impression.

The bailiff called the court to order. Lance Sterling noticed that his client's hands were shaking.

"Don't be nervous." Lance said. "I have a plan."

"I ain't nervous," Feldspar Quartz whispered in his ear. "My hands are shaking because I've been in jail for three days and I haven't had a drink the whole time. Hell, I ain't worried about the trial, the whole town thinks I'm a horse thief anyhow. I just hope they use a pretty rope, one that won't chafe my neck."

The judge entered the room and asked how the defendant pleaded.

Before Feldspar Quartz could say a word his attorney was standing beside his side and speaking for him.

"My client pleads 'Not Guilty, Your Honor," Lance said.

The audience gasped in shock. The jury looked startled; (most of them had other plans for the afternoon). The judge looked surprised and even Feldspar Quartz seemed a little bewildered by the plea.

"Call your first witness," the judge told the lawyer.

"My first witness is the oldest man in town." Lance Sterling said with a great big smile. After all, he had a plan.

Mr. Acorn, all hundred and eleven years of him shuffled up to the witness stand. The bailiff helped the elderly white-bearded man up to the witness stand.

The streets of Butte, Montana were honeycombed with mine shafts and ore tunnels. As a result from time to time a sidewalk would collapse or building fall into a new sinkhole. Even the courtroom was not immune from the dangers. A sinkhole had collapsed right in front of the witness stand, leaving a big dark pit whose bottom could not be seen. The citizens had offered to raise taxes and fix it but the judge kind of liked it; said it gave the witnesses something to think about as they placed a hand on the bible and "swore" to tell the whole truth and nothing but the truth if they could look down into the bowels of the earth while they were testifying.

Little white-haired Mr. Acorn managed to shuffle into the witness stand without falling into the pit. He was a hundred and eleven years old and in the year 1887 that meant he had been born the same year they wrote the Declaration of Independence.

The townsfolk said he had it memorized; the Constitution too.

"Mr. Acorn," the lawyer asked. "Do you think my client is guilty."

"Yep."

"What do you think of the evidence against him?"

"Pretty darn convincing," Mr. Acorn said.

"Do you remember that one 4th of July the two of us were fishing down by Carson Creek?"

"Yep," Mr. Acorn said. "Remember my advice — if you want to catch good fish you got to use good bait."

The jury and assembled courtroom audience chuckled.

"Do you remember the story you told me about circumstantial evidence not being allowed in a court of law?"

The old man smiled, he could see what Lance Sterling was up to.

"Why yes I do, it was one of my daddy's favorites," Mr. Acorn said proudly. "He was a judge you know."

"Could you tell us here in the courtroom today the story of "Circumstantial Evidence?"

"Certainly," Mr. Acorn said as he got up and bowed before the jury. "The story begins with a handsome young farm hand and a beautiful farmer's daughter. One day the handsome young farm boy was shoveling manure with a pitchfork in the barn, working hard in the hot humid summer, sweat glistening on the hard muscles. The farmer's daughter offered to quench his thirst with a pitcher of ice cool lemonade and some pleasant conversation.

The truth was that her sweet, pretty smile just made the young man's fire burn hotter and hotter. He kept on drinking just one more glass of lemonade, hoping she would stay just a little longer.

The farmer watched his daughter and the hired help get a little friendly and flirtatious. As a concerned father he could not help but dislike the notion so he made a move to end their romantic notions.

'Eliza,' he commanded, 'Back in the house!'

'And as for you young man,' he took the pitchfork out of the farm boy's hands and pointed the tines at him. 'Stay away from my daughter or you will soon see yourself unemployed.'

With the sharp points of the pitchfork only inches from

his face the young hired hand looked very frightened.

The farmer took the pitchfork away and put his arm around the scared boy. 'Now son, I know you're reaching that age when a boy has a lot of urges but you had better find an alternative solution to release that tension or you will lose your job. You go out and gather the cattle from the far pasture and bring them into the barn tonight before you eat supper. And stay away from my daughter!'

The far pasture was indeed far and the farm boy did not have all the cattle in the barn until long after sunset. By that time the farmer's daughter had fallen asleep; just the way the farmer had planned it. The hired hand led the farmer's prize calf in last but not least and with a weary sigh he had finished a day's work, long after it was night.

The farm boy was powerful hungry and couldn't wait to get up to the bunkhouse and eat his dinner, but there was one other biological need which needed to be taken care of first. It was because of all that lemonade. He was nearly overcome with the need to urinate. In his haste, the farm hand fumbled clumsily with his overalls; getting one side all the way undone but struggling and bumbling with the other one. At last he reached a point where he had finally gotten enough buttons undone where if he stood up on his tiptoes and leaned to the right with just enough stretch — he could pee.

Just in time too, the urge had become overwhelming. In his haste to satisfy his biological urge he had forgotten one important thing. He had left the barn door unlatched.

The prize winning calf was a mischievous animal and nudged the door with its nose before bolting for the far pasture and beyond just as the hired hand let loose a steady stream. The farm hand knew that if he did not stop the prize winning calf from escaping now he would not catch it until well past midnight. He would be very tired and extremely hungry by then. So he did the only thing he could.

Fast as lightning his hand shot out as the calf ran past, grabbing it by the last part he could; the very tip of the tail.

The calf stopped dead in his tracks but not without a powerful bleating, dragging the farm boy so that he had to dig in his heels.

The calf bleated louder.

The farmer was a prudent man and took good care of his livestock; not just out of kindness but motivated by profit as well. When he heard his prize winning calf bleating in such distress the farmer bolted out of bed, through the window and charged into the barn.

There he discovered the farm hand with his overalls about his ankles, his personal plumbing in one hand, and the tail of the bleating calf in the other.

You can imagine what the farmer was thinking; especially after talking with the boy about discovering alternative ways to relieve his urges but what he was thinking ain't necessarily so and the farm boy was not guilty of the crime the farmer was about to accuse him of."

The courtroom crowd chuckled, the jury laughed out loud, and the judge erupted into a series of roaring guffaws.

"And that, your Honor," Lance Sterling interjected. "Is why a man cannot be convicted with only circumstantial evidence."

The judge and jury were forced to agree. All the evidence was circumstantial and Feldspar Quartz was found innocent of horse thievery. Instead of a hanging and a barbecue the townsfolk were forced to settle for just a barbecue. The rarely sober Feldspar Quartz was a happy man.

The judge approached Lance Sterling, the lawyer, and shook his hand.

"That was an excellent defense sir," the judge said enthusiastically. "I don't think I ever heard better."

"Thank you," Lance Sterling said with a big smile, "Now I just have to find my client and collect my attorney's fees."

"Oh, didn't you notice?" the judge said. "He left town about an hour ago. I thought you knew about it because he rode away on your horse."

Bun in the Oven
Christine Rains

"Can ya feel him kickin'? He's gonna be strong like his Papa." Mary pressed her husband's hand against the great swell of her belly. She could hardly hold herself upright these days and all her dresses had to be widened using a cast iron cauldron as her manikin.

His head gave a stiff bob and blew out a long stream of smoke that trickled up the chimney to reach freedom. "He'll be a good lad, helpin' me out in the fields an' huntin'."

"Always outside. This is what it took for me to get ya in the kitchen!" Mary laughed and pat his pot belly. He opened his mouth to say something, but she suddenly put up a hand. "I hear horses in the distance." They both sat frozen for a few seconds and, indeed, there was the sound of someone approaching. "Stay in, stay hidden, sugar. Let me get rid of 'em."

Her husband open his mouth to protest, but Mary gave him a look that snapped his jaws shut. She smoothed her hands down over her swollen stomach and walked over to the door. With a quick look over her shoulder to make sure he was hiding, she stepped out onto the rickety porch. It creaked under her weight as if all that extra mass couldn't be just from the baby and she shushed it with a look similar to the one she flashed her husband just a moment ago.

Mary didn't smile as the three riders came to a halt in front of the little house. There were two trees guarding either side of her home, but they were scrawny and bent to the wind that blew in from the fields.

"Mrs. Whedon," the Sheriff eased down off his saddle and stood bow-legged as if he just finished his nightly visit at the brothel.

"Sheriff." Mary nodded her acknowledgment of his gruff greeting. "Doctor, Mr. Klein." She dipped her head to his two brothers, the town's doctor and banker.

"You're looking a bit pale today, Mrs. Whedon. How have you been feeling?" The doctor was the only one of the three without a mustache, but he ran his fingers over his upper lip as if he wore an invisible one.

"I'm fine. I'd come to town if I wasn't." Mary didn't move from her spot, but the porch creaked again. She stomped her heel on it for its insult.

"You know, it might be best if you come to town with us now. You're due any day now and with Frank havin' left—"

"Frank never left me." Mary snapped, chin in the air. "He's only gone workin'. He'll be back any day. I tole ya he sends me money. How else do ya reckon I'm feedin' this here baby in my belly?"

"Now, now," the Sheriff pat the muzzle of his horse as if it were a comfort to them all. "We talked about this before, Mrs. Whedon, an' we only were nice 'bout it considerin' your delicate condition, but you've got to be reasonable now. Frank ain't comin' back, darlin'. Let us take care of you."

Mr. Klein hopped up onto the porch from the far end. The bulge in his pants jiggled to demonstrate it was his money weighing him down no matter his other intentions towards her. "I have a room ready at my house for you. Let's just get your things and talk about this some back in town."

"You ain't welcome in my home, Mr. Klein. None of you Klein men!" Mary jabbed her finger at them and darted into the house, latching the door behind her. "Frank takes care of me. He'll be here. Jus' go back to your petty little lives, runnin' the town an' cheatin' workin' women from their just dues in more than one way. I'm fine where I am."

The other brothers joined the banker on the porch. She could hear them sigh with exasperation. Mary was more frustrated that she was angry and yet couldn't get a rise of them. The bastards had plagued her every few weeks like locusts coming back in hopes of a feast.

"Unlock the door, Mrs. Whedon. I don' want to have to break it on ya. This is for your own good, after all. Women in your condition don' think right." The Sheriff knocked on the door with a heavy hand. His foot echoed with an impatient tap and the fire in the stove crackled.

"Women in any condition don't think right." The banker added just loud enough for her to hear.

Mary gritted her teeth and looked back to make sure Frank was hidden. Perhaps if she let them take her to town, they wouldn't nose around the house and she could escape later on in the night to come back. Yet what if Frank needed her or if she went into labor in town? That wouldn't do at all.

As she scrambled with her thoughts, the Kleins showed no patience. A boot to the door flung it open and the latch flew across the room to land at the large feet of the iron stove. The door swung back and smacked the Sheriff so he stumbled backwards.

The doctor walked in first holding up his soft white

hands. "Don't get too worked up about this, Mrs. Whedon. It isn't good for the baby. Let me help you pack a few things and we'll be going. We'll go back to town and get you some cake. You can have the whole thing."

"Out! Out, out, out!" Mary's heart was racing in her chest. She grabbed her broom and attempted to shoo them out with it, swinging wildly like a mad yak tossing about its horned head. The stove puffed out more smoke.

She swung the broom at the Sheriff and he caught it deftly in his left hand with a smarmy smirk. He then pulled her to him with his right. "Calm down, darlin'. Come outside an' wait with me. My brothers will get what you need."

The banker had pulled out a bag from under her bed and opened it up. His brows furrowed and he sighed as he looked about the one room house. He stepped over to the wardrobe and opened it, going through the clothes she had stored there.

"Frank's comin' home! He won't like it when I tell him that you took me out of here 'gainst my will." Mary attempted to pull her arm free from the large man, but he only tightened his grip as he tugged her towards the door. "Let go! You can't hold me!"

"I almost can't with the size you are darlin'," he grunted. "Now, we all know Frank's never comin' home. He died out there makin' tunnels for the trains after he tunneled into you makin' that baby there." The Sheriff had an edge to his voice and dropped the broom as he caught her free hand when she tried to slap him. "You ain't been gettin' nothin' from him. No letters have come from through the express for ya. Whatever money you've got is jus' stashed an' it's gonna run out sooner than later. Let us take care of ya, darlin'."

Mary froze, staring at him with her mouth agape. "You've...been checkin' my mail? Spyin' on me?"

"We've been watchin' out for ya, Mary." The Sheriff's voice was softer yet gruffer with the use of her familiar name. "Come along now."

"No." She shook her head, trying to sit herself down on the floor as he pulled her towards the door. Her feet hissed along the floorboards to match the venomous glare she was giving her kidnapper. "No! I won't go, ya hear me? I'll never go with ya!"

The doctor came up from behind and urged her forward,

patting her rounded rump. "Stop this nonsense, Mrs. Whedon. You'll rile yourself up and disturb—"

Mary's cry of fury was echoed by a splash as her water broke and drenched not only her but the two Klein brothers as well. All of them looked down, silent except for the dribbling of her fluids.

"Oh my," the banker was the first to turn away with his face green with sickness rather than greed for the moment.

"See now, darlin', you worked yourself up an' now we've gotta rush you back to town." The Sheriff, taking advantage of her shock, scooped her up in his arms and headed out the door.

Mary finally came back to herself and tried to grab the door frame on the way out. "No! Stop! Put me down!" Tears streaked down her face and then she cried out with pain as she felt her first contraction.

There was a great squealing of iron and the pot bellied stove stood up. The Sheriff stopped just outside of the door with the porch shifting with a squawk. "What in the nine hells is that?"

The black legs of the stove straightened as the stack angled out to the side. There was more grinding of iron as two arms emerged from either side and a square head shaped like a kettle lifted from underneath the lid. It stood over seven feet tall and it had eyes that glittered like coal. Its jaw dropped open. "Mary!"

The banker promptly shat himself and slipped in his own mess as he tried to run.

The iron construct swung its left arm and flung the youngest Klein brother against the wall. He crumpled to the floor unconscious and stinking.

"Frank, no!" Mary kicked her legs to try to get away from her captor and to her husband's side.

"Frank?" the doctor squeaked, holding up his hands. "In the name of Heaven...." He backed away on quivering legs.

"Mary!" Frank's shout was a dry growl. Smoke poured from the stack in great dark clouds. The house quaked as he started forward. The second eldest Klein brother back away and underestimated the speed of the construct. Frank zipped forward and grabbed the doctor by the front of his jacket to shake him. "Leave my Mary alone!"

"Put him down, Frank. Put him down or I'll toss Mary

29

out into the yard." The Sheriff was the only brother not afraid of this thing. His mouth was set in a hard line.

"You wouldn't!" Mary shrieked and then cried out with another contraction. "He's comin' too fast! Oh, please God, Frank!"

"I would. Don't you doubt me." The Sheriff's gaze was firmly set upon Frank. "Now let him go and we'll talk about this. You know what I want, Frank. Give me what I want and I'll let Mary go."

"No, Frank!" Mary's round cheeks were wet and red. Her little fists hammered ineffectively at the big man that held her in his bruising grip.

Frank paused, seething with a hot hiss, and then threw the doctor behind him like a rag doll. The doctor landed against the table, turning it up on himself as he rolled over hard onto the floor. The table rolled a bit on the spot, but the man didn't even twitch.

"I put him down. Give me Mary." Frank marched forward with his iron hands closed into fists of cannon ball size.

The Sheriff stepped backwards near the stairs of the porch. He kept the pregnant woman in his arms between himself and her husband. "Give me the money, Frank. I know it's here."

Mary ceased her struggling and wrapped her arms around her bulging belly. She shook her head again and looked like a prickly cactus with locks of hair standing out in all directions.

"No, Sheriff. Money's gone." Frank's stack lowered more as he neared the front door. "Gave it to the scientist that saved me after the accident in the tunnel. Just had enough to tide Mary over 'til she had the baby."

"Saved you? Jesus, Frank, the devil put your soul into that thing an' it's the least you deserve for holdin' out on me. I'd wring your neck if you had one." The Sheriff grit his teeth. "I want the money, or your woman and the bun in the oven are mine. I might have a bit of fun with her, but in the end, she'll jus' be a cow to sell along with her calf."

Mary tried to hold back an anguished sob. Frank roared, echoing through his pot belly and stack. He rushed through the door like a runaway engine. The first foot he put onto the porch made a great crack, but there was no stopping his momentum. As the second foot along with his full weight was upon it, the porch collapsed. He fell forward to catch his wife and ended up like a turtle on his back.

The Sheriff had dropped the woman and fell backwards onto the dusty ground. His hat fell off and the sun nearly blinded the horses as it shone off the oldest Klein brother's head. The animals spooked and ran off down the road.

Mary had been saved by the cradle of her husband's arms, but had enough trouble trying to right herself never mind helping Frank up again. She groaned as she threw off planks of wood from them and tried to stand up. Frank's stack was blocked and smoke poured from his mouth, but he was heating up quick.

The Sheriff was faster onto his feet and scrambled over to the shed. He grabbed a pick from just inside the door and ran back towards the porch. "No one cheats me, Frank. Not even tin can bastards like yourself!" He brought the pick down and it glanced off the swell of the stove with a trail of sparks. He hit him again and again, finding weaknesses in the iron and joints to exploit.

Frank flailed in the dirt amongst the broken pieces of the porch, roaring with anger like a feral beast. The Sheriff howled with triumph as he pried open the door to the construct's inner workings.

A plank came crashing down over his bald head. His eyes rolled back and he fell down to the ground. Mary stood over him, breathing heavily, and spit on him. "A cow, my ass!"

"Mary." Frank had lost his roar and rolled to look at her, holding closed his belly's door.

"What do we do now, sugar? The baby's comin'. Can't stop him now." She unblocked his stack and touched his iron face with shaky but tender caress.

"Get the pryin' bar and help me up. I'll tie up the Kleins an' add some more fuel to my belly." Frank's jaw sat awkwardly for a moment, but he reached up to right it. "You prepare for the birthin'. We'll welcome our son an' then leave to go out west to California as a family. Jus' like we always planned. We'll sell the Kleins' horses for money for the trip an' a new house."

"You're still set on goin' out west, huh? At least you thought of everythin', sugar. I hope our boy here inherits some of your iron will." Mary smiled blissfully at him and fetched the metal bar from the shed to help him get to his feet.

Muleheaded
Will Morton

I'm riled with my fat worthless pony,
'Cos I figgered to save me some money.
An' his diet worked good,
I don't buy no more food.
But he lays an' won't move, bein' ornery.

Your Cows Are Out
Laura Finlay

"Your cows are out,"
I told him straight.
"You've let them stray outside the gate."

"What, ma'am?" he asked.
"What's that, you say?
My cows are safe at home today."

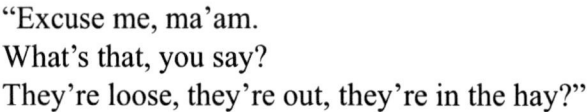

"Your steers are loose,
They're free to roam.
Please pen them in or call them home!"

"Excuse me, ma'am.
What's that, you say?
They're loose, they're out, they're in the hay?"

"No, no, cowboy,
Now, don't you fear.
You've failed to zip your Wranglers®, dear!"

The Truth
Paul Wittine

A tired cowboy
spends his days in the saddle
has a sore bottom

TROUBLE ON THE NORTH FORTY
Beth Lynn Clegg

The original premise for this work came from Bud Imhoff, the best story teller that ever walked the streets of Port Arthur, Texas. He agreed to my outrageous additions and editing before departing this world May 24, 2009.

This here's a story 'bout my hero, Coy Dodgers, and his wife, Gail Heavens. They live in a big ol' sprawling every-which-a-way house on two thousand acres of grazin' land that leaves plenty of roamin' room for a herd of registered jackasses and thoroughbred llamas. I got hired on as cook and handyman a ways back and look to end up my days right here.

But back to th' story. On this particular day, Coy was in th' living room of Th' Swankienda, that's what folks in these parts call it. He was spending another morning alone while Gail was tendin' to a sick friend twenty miles over on an adjoinin' spread. Tall, short, and medium sized gleamin' trophies from TV and movies look like they been scatter-shot into every nook and cranny. If I'm lyin' I'm dyin'. More framed awards than I can count cover up most of th' walnut paneled walls. Of course I could count 'em if I wanted to, I jest never wanted to. I mean, I didn't fall off a turnip truck on th' way out here. They got a room full of great big ol' furniture that's upholstered in hand cured llama hide. It just seems to beg a body to sink down and set a spell, or warm yer backside by th' huge fire burnin' in th' fireplace. You'd think that'd be more 'n enough to make a body happy.

Wellsir, that wasn't th' case. It dern sure wasn't intentional, but I was goin' in there to get somethin' when I overheard Coy through th' half open door. He's lettin' out big ol' sighs and talkin' to hisself about honey-do's. But it wasn't jest honey-do's had his dander up. He thought Gail was spendin' way too much time playin' nursemaid to their neighbor. Good friend, or not, she knew her first responsibility was takin' care of him. He was determined to up and tell her soon as she got home.

I jest stood there, quiet like, not knowin' what to do. At first I figgered he'd let up in a few minutes and I'd walk on in like I'd just got there. No way. I mean he'd built up a head of

34

steam that coulda fired a locomotive into action.

You see, besides being gone so much of late, Gail's endless chores had become a thorn in his side. Still, he hadn't come up with a way to talk about it that wouldn't set her off like stampeedin' cattle. Everyone on th' place knew she hadn't been herself in a coon's age. So he's sayin' things were bad enough without gettin' her riled up like an unbroke filly, and he wanted his sweet lovin' woman back. Stuff like that. Wellsir, after a bit more mutterin' he talked hisself out of it and decided to keep his trap shut a while longer. I could tell he was still agitated. I couldn't be sure but I figgered it had somethin' to do with th' dry spell that had hit his recordin' company.

Then, quick as snappin' yer fingers, he shook it off and turned to th' thing I love best. His music. He began strummin' th' guitar and fingerin' chords for an unfamiliar song. He was singin' most in a whisper sos I couldn't make out th' words.

All of a sudden, th' front door burst open and his trusted side-kick, Blabby Mayes, dashed into th' room. He's dirty, sweaty, and gaspin' for breath. Lookin' like a horse that's been rode hard and put away wet.

"What in th' name of Sam Hill's wrong with you, Blabby? Your slam-bang entrance ruined my mood. And I was singin' a song I was goin' to dedicate to you. So what thanks do I get? You almost made me drop my favorite guitar, that's what."

Without explanation or nothin', Blabby exploded in a torrent of words.

"Coy! A terrible thing jest happened! Rustlers cut th' fence on th' North Forty!"

Coy's body language changed in a jiffy. Anger and disbelief replaced his previous calm. He tossed th' guitar aside and beat a fist into his hand.

"Cut the fence, did they? Well those rustlers got to be stopped. They'll rue th' day they heard th' name, Coy Dodgers. I'll go saddle up Chigger."

But Blabby threw out an arm that sent Coy reeling back a couple of steps. I couldn't believe my eyes. Neither could Coy who barely managed, "What th'…"

"Sorry, Coy, but that ain't all. After they cut th' fence, they drove off all of your breeding jennies and most of your favorite stud jacks."

"Why th' dirty varmints! They won't get away with this!"

Coy strapped on twin holsters, checked to see if th' guns were loaded, and headed toward th' door.

This time Blabby grabbed him by th' shirt yellin', "Whoa there, Nellie!"

Now Coy was mad as a wet hen. He spun around to face Blabby. Ready for action. Body in a crouch. Fists lookin' like ham hocks.

"You gone plum loco on me, Blabby? What in tarnation's gotten into you? Pushin' and tuggin' on me like I'm some kinda rag doll. You tryin' to make me shoot myself in th' foot?"

"You know that ain't true, Coy! But that still ain't all. They done kidnapped Gail and said they was gonna rape her! What're we gonna do?"

With a look that sent chills up and down my spine, Coy strode to th' fireplace and took down a lever action rifle. He worked th' mechanism and put a couple of cartridges in th' chamber.

My eyes couldn't believe what they was seein'. We was gonna have us some action around here for a change! My hero was gonna save th' day! I was gonna have me a front row seat to th' biggest showdown Bluwit County ever seen.

"Those low down, good for nothin' varmints will pay for this, Blabby."

Those words weren't outta his mouth good when a horn started honkin' out front. Coy and Blabby got theirselves jammed up in th' doorway tryin' to be th' first one out. That was a sight, I tell you, but they was partially blockin' my view. Then I heard a voice that was music to my ears.

"Well, I must say, you two look mighty silly pressed up against each other like that," Gail said as she stepped outta a black shiny lemo stretching from here to Sunday.

"Gail! Honey! Are you all right?"

Finally freein' hisself from Blabby, Coy dashed to pick her up, and swung her around until she begged to be put down on th' porch.

Meanwhile, I'd slipped across th' room durin' all th' commotion. Peepin' out from behind th' curtains gave me a front row seat. It wasn't th' one I'd counted on earlier. That's for sure. Anyways, they jest rested for a short spell to catch their breath before Coy spoke up.

"Wait a minute. Where'd that lemo come from? You sure you're ok?"

"Coy! For gosh sakes! What's gotten into you? Of course I am. In fact, it's been a wonderful morning. Probably one of the best days I've had in years. The toughest part was keeping this whole thing secret from you all these weeks."

Coy's eyelids narrowed to slits. Jaw muscles rippled like a garden snake as he hissed at her through clenched teeth.

"Secrets? So that's how it is, is it? Been spendin' time takin' care of our "sick" friend, have you? Well, I get th' picture. I never thought I'd find myself married to a two-timin' woman."

"Coy Dodgers! I'd like to wash your filthy mouth out with soap! How dare you accuse me of being unfaithful? I asked Blabby not to tell you what was going on because I wanted it to be a surprise. Guess I should've known he'd do what he does best. Blab. But even if he did spill the beans, your undeserved reaction doesn't make any sense."

Coy starts to interrupt but she holds up a hand to silence him. For once, he backs down as she continues.

"I demand an apology. Now. Or I'm getting back in that lemo and heading into town. Maybe that'll give you time to get your head on straight."

"Don't try getting outta this by shifting th' focus to Blabby. He told me what was goin' on, alright. Rustlers cut th' North Forty fence, stole my asses, and took you off to gang rape you. I was just leavin' to put a few well placed slugs in th' varmints. Here you show up sayin' what a wonderful day it's been. What kinda fool do you take me for, Gail? You got no right to demand anything of me."

"Rape? I wasn't raped! A movie company leased our spread for a new western. I've had one of the best leading roles of my career. Everything's back in place like they promised. Fence's mended. Your precious asses are safe. They assured me I'd have a tape for a thumbs up or down before it's released. Blabby must've heard us talking about it. The tape's right here!"

"Come on. Don't josh me! That's not funny."

"You're right. It's not one bit funny. Here. Take the darned tape. You and your ridiculous jealousy have ruined everything."

"Tape? They were talkin' about a tape? Dadnabit,

Blabby! If I've told you once, I've told you a hundred times. Get a hearing aid!"

Blabby ducked his head, lookin' like a man prayin' a hole would open up and swallow him. He managed a few steps backward before Coy grabbed his arm.

"Oh, no you don't. You got me into this mess. You stay put until we get this straightened out."

Turnin' to Gail, with a hound dog look on his face, he began to sorta stammer. "I'd like, well, I'd really would like to hear about it. If you don't mind. And, if you have time. That is, if you plan to stick around."

"For your information, the movie's called, 'Trouble on the North Forty.' This was going to be a birthday surprise for you. I know you've been worried sick about the record company. Well, two of your songs are on the sound track, Coy. I thought you'd be thrilled, but now…"

"Two songs? There are two, count 'em, *two* of my songs on th' sound track? Well I'll be a sonofagun! I don't remember ever feelin' so dang foolish when I'm wantin' so bad to jump for joy. Seems as how we both owe you an apology, if you're willin' to listen."

"I don't know. To be perfectly honest, I'm disappointed in both of you. I'm trying to see how it looked after you heard Blabby's sordid tale. Then I show up in a lemo going on and on about my delightful day. Even so, I'm hurt. Bad hurt. You should've trusted me, Coy. I can't believe you didn't after all these years."

"I know, Honey. I've acted, like, what can I say? I musta gotten hold of a bad batch of loco weed! Come on. Tell me you're my lovin' woman, 'cause I'm you're ever lovin' man. Hey, now that might make a good song!"

Wellsir, they stood lookin' from first one to th' other for what seemed like forever. Felt like I was on the set of *High Noon.* Only difference was there were three people, 'stead of two, staring each other down. Waitin' to see who'd be th' first one to flinch.

Jest when I thought she was gonna get back in th' lemo and hightailit back to town, they all started huggin' an kissin' an carryin' on like crazy. I tell you, it was a sight for sore eyes before Coy finally reined 'em in.

"Whoa, there! What're we doin' out here? We got us some serious celebratin' to do! I don't know about you two, but I'm ready to see my birthday present!"

Now don't' that jest beat all? I mean he and Gail made up quicker 'n I can make a pan of biscuits. Yessirree! That's my hero for you!

WILD RIDE
Sarah Ashwood
For Bryan...

When I saw the old feller
He weren't much to see
I says to myself
"This nag cain't lick me."

So they hogtied him down
And I scrambled aboard
That horse took to jumping
Like kids on a board

That nag went straight up
Then crashed right back down
I let out a shout
Heard all over the town

He crawfished and leapt
Did a nice barrel roll
I clung like a spider
And prayed for my soul

Up off of all fours
We sailed in the air
Came down with a jolt
Knocked my hat from my hair

But I held on to him
He couldn't knock me off
That devil-spawned jackass
What passed for a hoss

My bunk was too hard
For sleeping that night
My aches and my pains
Were a terrible fright

I cursed him for hours
Unable to sleep
While snug in his stall
He made not a peep

Next day I was wonderin'
As I hurt mightily
"Did I tame that horse —
Or did that sucker tame me?"

The Hand You're Dealt
K.C. Ball

Come listen to my story,
from days of gold and glory,
when the fastest way to travel was by train.
Lots of folks were heading west,
putting fortune to the test;
with a lot to lose and even more to gain.

Now the trip could last for days,
and a traveler needed ways,
to keep from getting God-Almighty bored.
Some told stories, a few read,
Some dreamed dreams inside their head;
Others gambled for what stakes they could afford.

Now on one such trip, I'm told,
were six fellows seeking gold,
but they weren't miners; their kind favored suits.
They'd got up a little game,
table stakes, just sort of tame;
still they watched each others' hands need sleeves and boots.

They were playing five-card stud,
dealt out by One-Eyed Bob,
When the door to the compartment opened wide.
Oh, the festive mood was altered,
and their easy laughter faltered;
the conductor of the westbound stepped inside.

He announced, "You men aren't fools,
you all know the railroad's rules;
No gambling is permitted on this train.
But I take the easy view,
so let me sit in, too,
and I'll let you start this friendly game again."

What could they do but nod?
This man was next to God,
when it came to judgments while upon the rail.
So they all said, "What the heck."
And Bud handed him the deck,
but his presence at the table cast a pall.

And when he started dealing,
the men couldn't shake the feeling,
there was something not quite kosher with his work.
Soon all of them were mumbling,
but the point of all their grumbling,
at last was voiced by Dapper Bobby Kirk.

"If you didn't run this train,
our options would be plain,
for I saw you deal that clumsy, cheating hand.
But I'll tell you what we'll do,
we'll just turn the trick on you;
and upset the little scam that you had planned.

So you toss those cards away,
they won't see the light today.
We'll watch you deal yourself a brand-new lot,
Then we'll sit and play this game,
with the angry sounding name,
until we settle just who wins the pot.

Well, friends, you all can bet,
that that conductor's brow was wet,
when he finally settled back into his chair.
And those six around him smiled,
for they saw the he was riled,
'bout playing out his new cards fair and square.

So this fat man, name of Ned,
peeked at his cards and said,
"I'll start the betting with a big blue chip."
Now, those blues were worth one hundred,
so the others should have wondered,
"Is a bet against Fat Ned a sinking ship?"

But Joe Bob looked at his hand,
and he smiled and said, "My man,
I just have to see that blue and raise you two!
'Cause I've got five righteous cards,
and I have to tell you, pards,
that with this hand I feel real bad for you."

The others at the table,
as soon as they were able,

41

commenced to throw more blues upon the felt.
The heat of all the betting,
soon had those fellows sweating,
but their cold eyes wouldn't make soft butter melt.

That private car was steaming,
as each man sat there dreaming,
of the fortune, fame and glory in his hand.
Not a man jack drew or dropped,
so that when the betting stopped,
the middle of the table held ten grand.

The players turned to Ned,
whom they'd called, and so he said,
"I've got a full house, seven over ten."
"That's a winning hand," he thought,
but Ned's heart sure bumped a lot,
when he saw the greedy smiles upon the men.

One by one, they fueled the fire,
each a full house, only higher,
until there was a dreadful, deadly hush.
The conductor wore a grin,
as he threw his pasteboards in,
ten through ace of hearts. He had a royal flush.

So, friends, that there's my story,
from the days of gold and glory,
when the fastest way to travel was by train.
But on board you best not bet,
'gainst the house, 'cause all you'll get,
is an empty wallet, and that's right as rain.

SADDLE PAL
Jim Cardwell

We first encountered the problem when one day old Charlie Smyth
got to thinking about the things he hadn't done with his life.
And when a cowboy gets to thinking about mortality
you never know what might happen or what the outcome could be.
He'd been working for outfits since a scrapping lad in his teens
and never worried much about saving for his future means.

Last year at a county fair he stopped to watch a puppeteer
observing how ventriloquists move a hand, an eye, an ear.
For many weeks those images kept running around in his head.
Then armed with faded flannel long johns, buttons, needles and thread,
he fashioned the first of half a dozen fabricated pards.
One by one those shifty saddle pals slickered us off our guards.

He finely crossed the border line of simple saddle shows
when he mail ordered to New York where puppet building pros
built a pint sized cowboy puppet designed to look just like him
with a handle bar mustache and deceptively friendly grin.
"Billy" arrived in a padded box that locked both high and low.
Charlie's one day needing the same was something we'd yet to know.

Both signed on to work Alturus through the summer and the fall
practicing the skills they would need to play at Carnigge Hall.
Now Charlie is a cowboy true. He's honest, brave, and gallant.
But as for ventriloquism, he sadly lacks the talent
Our first night out, around the fire with one man singing low
Charlie unbuckled Billy and started putting on a show.

They both wore faded Wrangle jeans with a long sleeved flannel shirt.
A new grey Stetson, buckskin boots. Not a smudge of trail dirt.
This quickly caught our attention. We stopped and watched a while.
The two of them looked so alike, at first we just had to smile.
But a hitch became apparent that got us all to gawking.
We were never really sure which dummy was doing the talking.

Charlie's lips would move, his face contort, his Copenhagen leak
every time, or so we thought, it was Billy trying to speak.
And they really weren't that funny. Much too personal too,
It got to wearing thin when they started talking about you.
There were a couple arguments, and it could have caused a fight
until the boss intervened and turned us all in for the night.

In the evenings following, when we'd normally socialize,
Charlie would sometimes sneak out Billy and take us by surprise.
He'd joke about me. He'd joke about you. Anyone at all.
This would become unbearable if it lasted until fall.
Hands started riding night herd and doing unsavory tasks.
If it wasn't with those two jokers, you didn't have to ask.

We thought it odd when one day the boss sent Charlie into town
to get supplies we needed, and new duds for his wooden clown.

Once out of sight he called us all in and a meeting was swiftly held
so everyone could speak their mind.
Some grumbled. Some begged. Some yelled.
Billy would cut you where you hurt. The pain was hell to feel.
We finally got to believing that Billy was live and real.

Now, I ain't one for murdering, so Charlie Smyth could live.
But as for that New York City menace, something had to give.
Convincing us to rise and act, the boss didn't have to try.
The only question now was how soon would Billy die?
The very next night with supper done, the boss to Charlie said
"Why not give us all another show before we're off to bed?"

That's all it took to bait the hook. We sat up straight and sturdy.
I whittled as Jose braided. The boss cleaned his 30-30.
From the darkness came pounding hooves. A branch snapped off a tree.
A voice from behind the wagon yelled, "A horse is running free."
The show came to a sudden halt. Two men ran to inquire.
The boss ejected two cartridges into the blazing fire.

"Jump for cover!" Jose hollered. I pushed Charlie off his seat
leaving Billy sitting much too close to the glowing, deadly heat.
One shell exploded! Then the other! Sparks and stuffing scattered.
None of us was shot or burned. And that's what mostly mattered.
We raised our heads up carefully. Charlie called out Billy's name.
His saddle pal lay face down burning, feeding the fire's flame.

Jose cried out, "I couldn't move. My Wranglers snagged on that stump.
I knew I was a dead man. And that's when I saw Billy jump.
He saved my life, and maybe yours. I know I'm sounding insane.
Except for that New York puppet, I'd be in a heap of pain."
There was no doubt. Billy was dead. Charlie just left him lay.
Every hand just hung their head. No one dared to walk away.

Now, all of this was carefully planned. Of that they're no denying.
Strange thing is, I saw Billy jump too! And I'm not one for lying.

THESE BOOTS AIN'T MADE FOR WALKIN'
Patricia Wellingham-Jones

He teeters, the dude from New Jersey,
balanced in first cowboy boots.
With sudden lurch and a sideways grab
he falls over — to onlookers' hoots.

Safely astride the broken-down mare
his pointy toe rakes horse's ribs.
In search of stirrup his boot slides right
through. Poor horse wonders what gives.

Up trail, then down, bottom bouncing,
dude prays for the ride to end.
Topples from mare, picks up his hat,
staggers off, worries how soon he'll mend.

HOW THE WAIST WAS LOST
Danny Birt

The blazing sun of high noon shone down on the two men facing off on Main Street.

'Dusty' Dustin held his hand at his waist, a mere inch from his pistol's handgrip. He wiggled his fingers slightly to keep himself ready for any sign of his opponent's intentions.

The man in the black hat twitched his fingers toward his own pistol in response, as if to tease Dusty into going for his gun.

The people inside the saloon were watching the tense duel carefully, afraid of what the outcome might mean for them.

Dusty suddenly drew his **gum** and pointed it at the man in the black hat.

The man in the black hat shot him through the heart.

As he fell to the ground dying, Dusty's last thought was, "Stupid editor. How could you not notice the difference between an 'N' and an 'M?'"

Go Ahead, Make My Day
Paul Wittine

Outlaw Josey Wales
star of spaghetti westerns
Mayor of Carmel

Law West of the Miskatonic
Whitt Pond

I'd just finished cleanin' out the spitoons when...

Sorry. I shoulda said cuspidors. The Judge insists on callin' 'em cuspidors. Says it's more refined, like what Miz Lilly would call 'em if'n she was here.

Anyways, I'd just finished cleanin' out the cuspidors when the Sheriff...

No. Sheriff Smith done got hisself kilt last year tryin' to bring in the Whateley twins. A-yeah. Over near Dunwich Gulch a'ways. All we ever found was a big burnt black spot, like what lightnin' struck, and a buncha melted horseshoes. We figger them belonged to the horse, since they wouldna' fit Sheriff Smith no-how.

The new sheriff? Big Bob Howard's been sheriff fer 'bout three months now. A-yeah. From over in Cross Plains. No, no, he's fine now. Best sheriff we ever had. Just don' say nothin' 'bout his mama, okay?

Anways, like I was sayin', I'd just finished cleanin' out the cuspidors when Sheriff Howard a'came in with Buck Robinson and The Lurker and two dead fellers a'strung across a mule (the dead fellers, that is, not Buck or The Lurker). There was a crowd a'foll? in' him, includin' the Widder Bertie West who looked fit to be tied.

"Howdy, Sheriff," I says as he come up to the Lilly. A-yeah. The Jersey Lilly. We was gonna call it the New Jersey Lilly, on account of it bein' new and all, but the Judge didn' like the sound of that, so we just kept it the Jersey Lilly, and if'n the folks in Langtry or Vinegaroon don' like it, they can come and take it up with the Judge.

"Howdy, Augie," the Sheriff says back as he hitches the mule to the rail outside the Lilly, ignorin' the crowd. And the Widder West, which ain' the easiest thing in the world. "The Judge in?"

"A-yeah," I says, lookin' the prisoners over. Buck was only handcuffed, but he didn' look like he was inclined to run off. Looked kinda sorrowful, truth be told, but that coulda been just 'cause his head was a hangin' that way, his neck bein' broke 'n all. And the two dead fellers wasn' likely to be goin' off nowhere neither, bein' as how they was fresh dead and not walkin' dead.

The Lurker, now, it was tied-up real good. Which was good as it kept a strugglin' and a hissin' and givin' everyone baleful glares outta them big yeller eyes it has all over. It seemed to take a special dislikin' to me, 'cause the next thing I knowed it was a'spittin' somethin' black and vile right where I was a'standin'.

Lucky fer me, I had them cuspidors in hand, and so I catched the stuff right quick—what with the Judge's spittin' aim not bein' so good, I'd had a lotta practice—and didn' get none on me. Which I can tell you was a good thing on account o' it started eatin' through the cuspidor bottom almost afore I could drop the thing.

Now everyone in New Arkham knows Sheriff Howard don' take kindly to spittin' in public, so it don' surprise no one when he turns and whomps The Lurker with his rifle butt right twixt its topmost set of eyes. The Lurker took to howlin' and shakin' its tentyculls, but when the Sheriff raised his butt up again it got peaceable 'n quiet real quick-like.

"Augie," Sheriff Howard says to get my attention—I was a'starin' at where the black stuff comin' outta the cuspidor bottom was eatin' into the ground—"go tell the Judge I got him three cases what need dealin' with at his convenience."

"Yessir," I says, backin' up into the saloon. I wasn' needin' no extry excuse to get outta range in case The Lurker commenced to spittin' again.

The Judge was behind the bar, as usual, arguin' with Boston Dick Pickman. You know. That artist feller from back east what always goes round wearin' a bowler 'n gloves. No, I don' recollect ever seein' him playin' cards.

Anyways, the Judge was all red-faced and lookin' ready to spit, which always happens when he gets to arguin' with Boston Dick. I puts the remainin' cuspidor on the floor and stays quiet, knowin' better than to interrupt the Judge when he's holdin' forth on Miz Lilly.

"And I'm a tellin' you I don' *want* no Shoggoths in the back-ground!" the Judge snarls, so mad his beard's a'quiverin' like an albino rattler's tail. "And no Shub-Nigguraths neither! Just paint 'er the way she's a'shown on this here poster-bill."

Boston Dick is holdin' a canvas up on the bar, his mustache a'sweatin' he's so nervous. "It... it's cahled ahtistic license, yooah Honah. I'm shooah yooah bah will—"

No, the Judge wasn' holdin' a gun in his mouth! That's just the way them Boston fellers talk, is all. Don' matter how he said it, though. The Judge wasn' havin' none of it.

"I don' recall issuin' you a license, artistic or otherwise," the Judge says, shovin' the canvas back at Boston Dick. "But if I don' have a proper paintin' of Miz Lilly to hang over the bar by noon tomorrow, I *am* gonna issue some licenses for tarrin' 'n featherin'! Now git!"

After Boston Dick done git—a'mutterin' 'bout filly-steens, whatever them is—I lets the Judge know Sheriff Howard's back.

"I don' suppose he brung in the Whateley twins this time?" the Judge scowls, still a'fumin' over the big blank spot behind the bar where his paintin' of Miz Lilly was s'posed to be.

"No, yer Honor. But he says he does got three cases that need judicatin'."

"Oh he does, does he?" The Judge glances at me, his black eyes a'glitterin' all displeased-like, and I remember the proprieties. No judicatin' till the last payin' customer's played out or passed out. I take my hat off real quick-like, addin' "Uh, at yer convenience, he says."

The Judge nods, the dignity of the court 'n saloon satisfied. "Tell Bob to set 'em up and I'll be over directly."

"Yessir, yer Honor," I says, backin' out and keepin' my hat off.

"And tell him to mind the billard table this time, 'lessen he wants to buy me another one!"

48

It was gettin' on to 'round three o'clock, when the Judge finally finishes servin' the last customer. I was gettin' kind of anxious. The court side of the saloon done filled up early and some of the patrons was startin' to sober up again.

"The bar is closed," the Judge announces, foldin' his saloon apron, "'cept of course for medicinal emergencies that come up and customers payin' in silver." Taking down his ol' alpaca coat from the leftmost rack of deer antlers, the Judge crosses over to the court side of the saloon. "Call 'em to order, Bob."

Sheriff Howard had just finished rollin' a cigarette. He looks at it kind of wistful-like, then tucks it in his vest pocket as he stands and clears his throat.

"Ever'one on yer feet." Glancin' at the tentyculls sprawlin' out from one end of the defendants' box, he adds "or whatever you got fer feet."

"Hear-ya, hear-ya," he calls out as the Judge finishes buttonin' his coat, "the first and onliest court of New Arkham is now in se-shun. The honorable Judge Roy Bean presidin'."

Standin' behind the bench, the Judge surveys the courtroom, his *1879 Revised Statutes of Texas* under one hand and his Colt Peacemaker under the other. Fortunately everyone was standin', though Frankie Long was needin' some assistance, passed out as he was. The Sheriff and I breathes a mite easier when the Judge finally sits hisself down, lettin' everyone else sit too.

"What d'you got fer me today, Bob?"

"Well, first we got a People versus..." the Sheriff pauses to look at the back of a medicine drummer's handbill where he'd scribbled some notes. "...Bill Briden and Gus Johansen, Two Durned Fools What Got Shot Dead Tryin' To Cheat At Cards." He nodded over at the old billiard table – Judge didn' allow bodies on the new billiard table – where the two miscreants were stretched out.

A-yeah. A-yeah. I'm a'comin' to that. Well, you musta been *some* kinda miscreant, else you wouldn' a'ended up dead and stretched out a on a billard table in the Lilly, now would you?

Anyways, quit interruptin'. It ain' polite.

Now the Judge is famous for comin' to quick decisions,

his bein' the finest legal mind west of the Miskatonic. So it didn' take longer than one good spit for him to announce his verdict.

"I hereby fine the defendants..." The Judge looks over to me, once I'm finished goin' through the dead fellers' pockets. "How much they got on 'em, Augie?"

"This 'un had about ten in silver, yer Honor," I says, lookin' apologetical. "The other 'un only had six bits."

"Fair enough," the Judge says, slammin' the bung hammer down on the bench, barely missin' a cockroach. "I hereby fine the defendants ten dollars 'n six bits for disturbin' the peace..."

"As I recollect," Sheriff Howard says, glancin' over sidewise and givin' me the hairy eyeball, "that other'un had two gold teeth."

Hey, don' blame me none! It were the Sheriff what mentioned it. And anyways, you *did*!

"...and a further ten dollars in gold teeth for practicin' dentistry without a license," the Judge says without a hitch, slammin' the bung hammer down again, this time with a right satisfyin' splat. The Judge pauses to give me a hairy eyeball of his own, then looks back to the Sheriff. "What do we got next, Bob?"

"Well, next we got a People versus Buck Robinson."

"Buck Robinson?" The Judge frowns, lookin' over at Buck real thoughtful-like. "Didn' we hang you last week?"

"Yes, yer Honor." Buck tries to nod, but with his broke neck it comes off more like a wobble. "You sure did."

"Horse-stealin', wasn' it?"

"Yes, yer Honor. That and, uhm..." Buck takes to scratchin' his head, which I tell you looked right peculiar, it stickin' out all sidewise like it was. "Po... puz..."

"Possesshun of stolen goods," Sheriff Howard says, readin' from the back of his handbill again.

"That's the one," Buck says, his head a'wobblin' eagerly. "What Bob says, yer Honor,"

"And was you guilty?" the Judge asks.

"Guilty as sin, yer Honor," Buck says, lookin' like he'd have his hat in his hands, if'n he'd had a hat, which he didn't.

"So who's tryin' to overturn my verdict?" The Judge looks back to the Sheriff, but Sheriff Howard just kind of shrugs and nods over at where the Widder West is sittin', next to the court's stuffed bear. The Judge frowns all twisty-like, lookin' like a man about to swaller a scorpion tail-first.

"Bertie West, approach the bench."

A-yeah. That's her. Hair like dead grass, face like someone put a pair o' spectyculls on a hatchet. You ain'? Well, you'll be findin' out directly.

Anyways, the Widder West a'gets up—right lady-like if'n anyone that hard-boned and hard-minded can be thought of as lady-like—and stands in front of the Judge.

"Bertie West," the Judge says, his eyes a'glintin' like two chips of obsidian off'n an Apache war-knife, "you been reanimatin' again?"

"Yes, yer Honor." The Widder's a'glarin' back at him, all bug-eyed through the spectyculls, and the way she says "yer Honor" you can tell she means "you low-down, no-account, booze-swillin' sonofa—"

No, I ain' embellyshin'! Just look over there at the way she's a'lookin' at you. A-yeah. Tender as a barbed-wire saddle on a salt lick.

So anyways, the two of 'em just kinda glare at each other like a coupla fightin' cocks with their hackles all up. But finally it's the Judge what blinks, and the next thing I knowed he's a'reachin' under the bench.

Now everyone in New Arkham knows the Judge only keeps two things under the bench, and one of them's this scattergun what he pulls out for 'difficult cases'. So I dives right quick-like under the billiard table—no, the new one—and most everyone else is a'duckin' and a'scramblin', except for Sheriff Bob and Frankie Long who's done passed out again. Even The Lurker is a'duckin', his hind tentyculls a'wavin' over the defendants box like a bouquet o' rat tails. And truth be told, I even saw the Widder back up a step.

But when the Judge sits up again, it's just his fortifyin' bottle that he's a'bringin' up, so everyone kinda goes back to their seats all sheapish-like. Me, I stays under the billiard table.

"Dammit, Bertie," the Judge fumes, pourin' hisself a glass, "the weddin' vows clearly state 'Till death do you part'." After a quick fortifyin', he sets down the glass with a thunk and glares at the Widder again. "You and Buck there is legal parted."

51

"Well, I un-parted us," the Widder says. "I ain' hardly had him long enough to try him out." Then she folds her arms acrost her chest real stubborn-like and fixes her eye—the left 'un—right on the Judge. "And I ain' gonna give him up just 'cause you was fool enough to get your horse stole while you was a'bundlin' with Mercy Tillinghast!"

"That's irrelevant contempt o' court!" the Judge shouts, bangin' the bung hammer down and a'grabbin' up the Peacemaker, "felonious libel, and treason agin' the bench!"

So everyone's a'divin' fer cover again. 'Ceptin' me 'cause I'm still under the billiard table. And Sheriff Howard, who's approachin' the bench real careful-like.

"Yer Honor," he says, keepin' his voice all calm 'n soothin'—and keepin' hisself twixt the Judge and the Widder, which ain' the healthiest place to be— "I think what we got here is a case o' extenuatin' circumstances."

"What kind o' extenuatin' circumstances," the Judge mutters, tryin' to draw a bead on the Widder, which is a problem 'cause she's a lot smaller than the Sheriff and quicker'n a six-legged jackrabbit to boot.

"It's a matter o' some discreshun, yer Honor," the Sheriff says, givin' the Judge a kind of a knowin' nod. "If'n I might approach the bench a mite closer?"

The Judge ain' been able to get a clear shot, so he nods and the Sheriff comes up and whispers in his ear whilst the Widder keeps herself outta his direct line 'o sight.

Now I cain' hear what the Sheriff's a'tellin' the Judge, but it ain' all that hard to guess. The town *did* promise the Widder a new husband if'n she'd do some reanimatin' for us. A-yeah. You got it. Well, he wasn' doin' nobody no good just a'lyin' there in the Langtry cemetery. And the town did need a judge.

"I see," the Judge says, lookin' like he did finally have to swaller that scorpion. He sets the Peacemaker down and sets his hand back on the bung hammer. "Bertie West, it seems the court does have some obligations to you in the matter of your matrimonial status."

Now the Widder is a'lookin' like a coyote what got into the hen house on a Saturdy night, and Buck is a'lookin' like one of the hens. But the Judge, he ain' a'finished yet. Not by a Texas mile.

"But the law is the law." The Judge straightens his alpaca coat all formal-like and turns to Buck. "Buck Robinson, I hereby pronounce you a free man," he says, slammin' the bung hammer down, "the re-hangin' to take place by sundown. Soon's the court's closed and you've had a chance for a farewell drink or two."

"Thank-ya, yer Honor," Buck says, lookin' grateful enough to cry. "Thank-ya kindly."

The court starts a cheerin' and a clappin' Buck on the back, and the Widder looks fit to bust a gut. But before she can start the Judge bangs the court to order again.

"Like I said, the court does recognize its obligations," the Judge says, lookin' over at the Widder. "So if'n you'll settle down and hold your peace, I'll see to that directly."

The Widder don' look too convinced, but she sits down anyways, next to the stuffed bear again. But all the men in the court what ain' been hitched are startin' to look a mite nervous. And the way the Widder commences to lookin' 'em over, I ain' a'comin' out from under that billiard table till New Year's.

"Bring on yer last case, Bob," the Judge says, takin' another sip of fortifyin'.

The Sheriff stands up and motions at The Lurker, and it kinda rises up too. No, I don' rightly know how, seein' as it ain' got feet to speak of, but it rised up anyways.

"Well, yer Honor," the Sheriff says, bringing out his handbill again, "last we got us a People versus The Lurker, What Has Been Mutilatin' Cattle, Consortin' With The Unnameable, And..." he looks over at The Lurker real unpleasant-like "Ruinin' The Fishin' In Miskatonic Creek."

"I see," the Judge says, givin' The Lurker a dark look o' his own, bein' partial as he was to fishin' and the Miskatonic havin' the only decent fishin' in fifty miles. "Lurker, you got anythin' to say in your defense?"

The Lurker commences to a moanin' and wavin' its tentyculls about— them what ain' tied down anyways—its yeller eyes all a rollin' real baleful-like. I don' rightly know. A'callin' on them Elder Gods, I suppose.

"Out of order and objecshuns overruled," the Judge shouts, a'bangin' the hammer loud as he can, but The Lurker keeps right on a'moanin' and carryin' on. Till the Judge reaches for his Peacemaker, that is. Then the Lurker quiets down real sharp-like.

"Lurker," the Judge says, "I hereby find you guilty of despoilin' private property, of ruinatin' public waters, and..." the Judge ponders the matter a moment, then adds "and of generally bein' contrary to existence as laid out by God in the state of Texas."

Now the court got real quiet. Everybody knowed the Judge is real partial to hangin', but The Lurker ain' got no neck. So we was real curious as to how the Judge was gonna handle it. But it turns out, the Judge had somethin' else altogether in mind.

"Now, bein' as how this is your first offense," the Judge says, a'strokin' on his beard all thoughtful-like, "the court has decided to rehabilitate you. So I'm a givin' you a choice: sworn or hitched."

The Lurker's eyes kinda blink all at once and it makes a noise that sounds somethin' like it don' understand. Which it probably didn' 'cause I was right puzzled myself.

"What I'm a'sayin'," the Judge says, "is that you can either swear on as deputy to Sheriff Howard over there," he nods over to where the Sheriff is lookin' kinda startled-like "till such time as you get kilt or you 'n him bring the Whateley twins in."

"Or," the Judges goes on, "you can serve the court by gettin' hitched to the Widder West," he points the bung hammer over to where the Widder is givin' The Lurker a powerful lookin' over "seein' as how her un-parted husband is about to be re-deceased."

Now, it's hard to say, the Lurker not bein' rightly human 'n all, but you could kinda tell it was in a quandry, a'twistin' back 'n forth twixt the Sheriff and the Widder. I kinda felt sorry for it, 'specially when its hind tentyculls took to tremblin' and one of its eyes popped out.

"So, what's it gonna be?" the Judge says, a'takin' out his pocket watch and eyein' the time.

Why? 'Cause it was a'gettin' close to five, which is when the Judge generally closes the court and opens the bar again. Barely enough time to do both a swearin' and a hitchin'.

No, I mean both. See, The Lurker, it done decided it'd rather go up agin' the Whateley twins than be hitched to the Widder West. So it goes over real meek-like, and Sheriff Howard unties it so's it can raise its right tentyculls—I don' know, 'bout half a dozen or so—and get sworn in by the Judge. A-yeah, it's Deputy Lurker now. Even Sheriff Howard is startin' to cotton to the idea.

The Widder? Well, see, this is why the Judge is the finest legal mind west of the Miskatonic. He don' let nothin' go to waste. Once The Lurker done decided to get deputized, the Judge turns to the Widder.

"Bertie, seein' as how you're still short a husband, you can take yer pick of the two fine gentlemen a'layin' on the billiard table over there."

A-yeah. 'Fraid so. Well, she *is* a reanimater.

Why you instead of the other'un?

Probably them gold teeth.

BUSTIN' A BRONC
Will Morton

"Git up!" hollered Jake, "Dawn's a-makin'
Them broncos is ready fer breakin'!"
But he sang, 'long 'bout noon,
Quite a diff-er-ent tune,
Sayin', "This ol' behin' be a-achin'!"

THE LONESOME RIDER
Timothy A. Sayell

For my Uncle Kelley, who always liked cowboy stories.

The sun was shining on the sage,
The rocks, and on the sand.
It did its very best, indeed,
To brighten up the land,
From the mountains, 'cross the prairies
To the streams where gold was panned.

Two horses raced across the arid plains, kicking up dust in their wake. The first horse was white as driven snow. It was strong and lean and carved a path through the sparse scrub with certainty and determination. The rider on its back was likewise dressed in white from his boots to his ten-gallon hat, save the silver six-gun hanging from his black belt, the embroidered roses on his shirt, the red bandana around his neck, and his black mask.

The second horse was brown and trod the desert plain with familiar ease and sure-footed grace. The rider of this horse, a noble-faced Indian with black hair down to his shoulders, was clad in simple buckskins. A beaded headband encircled his chiseled brow, and a pair of feathers stuck up from the back, almost like a pair of rabbit ears. He also wore a gun at his waist, as well as a knife, and a bow was slung across his back, a quiver of arrows hung from the saddle.

Before long, the pair found a set of railroad tracks. They looked in both directions, but saw no sign of a nearby town. After a brief debate, the man in white pulled out a silver dollar and flipped it. Following the will of happenstance, the pair followed the tracks into the low foothills. The sun rose higher in the sky as they followed the tracks, and they did not stop until they found the woman. She was beautiful, with red hair and bright eyes, and securely tied to the rails.

The man in white brought his horse to a stop, tipped his hat politely and said, "Mornin', ma'am."

The woman looked up at the pair with trepidation then glanced at her bag, unguarded, sitting by the tracks. "Are you robbers?"

"No ma'am!" the cowboy replied.

She breathed a sigh of relief. "In that case, if you'd be good enough to move along. I'm a bit tied up this morning..." she said as she struggled with the thick ropes.

"I noticed that," said the cowboy. "Is that one of them fancy new weight-reducing techniques or something?"

She grunted with effort as she vainly pushed and pulled against the tight knots. "If you must know, I was trussed up this-a-way by a nefarious banker and if I can't come up with the mortgage payment by five o'clock, his bank will own my ranch! So, you can see that I've no time for gabbing, I've got to get myself off these tracks and raise some money!"

The man in white looked at his Indian companion, who shrugged, then turned back to the woman on the tracks. "Sorry to be a pest, ma'am. Could you tell us how much farther it is to the next town?"

"You're just outside of Dehydrated Gulch," said the redhead, "You can follow the train tracks and get there in about two hours, but it's only about a half hour from here, as the crow flies."

The Indian grunted. "We not go by crow," he said. "How long it take on horse?"

"Same half hour," she said, squirming beneath the ropes. "If you go in the right direction." Then a sudden thought sparked a gleam in her eye. "Why, if you two would be good enough to cut little ol' me out of these ropes, I'd be pleased to point ya'll towards town."

"Fair enough. Duck, get out your knife and cut the lady loose."

"Okay, Kemo-Slobby!" said the Indian as he dismounted. He pulled out his knife and quickly cut through the ropes. He helped the lady to her feet and walked her over to the horses, grabbing her bag and handing it to her on the way.

"What a relief!" she sighed. "I was sure the noon train was gonna catch me, it's always about an hour early!"

"Hmm, me check," said the Indian as he lay down facing them, his back to the tracks, and pressed his ear against the dusty ground. A whistle blew nearby as a locomotive rounded the bend and sped past them. It pulled a dozen cars behind it, and was followed by a trio of mean-looking horsemen who yelled and fired wildly in the air, all this was trailed by a handcar manned by a pair of hobos. The Indian climbed to his feet and slapped away the dust as he shook his head authoritatively. "Train is much far away. Wheel on baggage car need oil, slow up whole trip."

"Oh, well thank you both!"

"Not at all, ma'am, it's what I do. I'm the Lonesome Rider, and this is my faithful friend, Sitting Duck," the masked horseman declared in a strong voice.

"Oh!" said the woman in a breathless voice. "You're who? Never mind, it doesn't matter. I'm Suzannah Sweetly, and I inherited the Double-Uno when my poor old father died in a common, everyday accident involving a runaway buggy, an outhouse, fourteen barrels of molasses, a stampede of jackrabbits, and that terrible cactus that they could not fully remove in time for the funeral." She sniffled sadly. "They tell me it happens all the time." She pulled a hanky from her bag and dabbed at her eyes.

The Rider deflated sadly on his horse. "How can you have not heard of me?" he brokenly asked. "I'm famous over in Empty Well…Mesa Flats…Big Butte…"

"The quickest way to Dehydrated Gulch is that-a-way, right over those hills," Suzannah said as she pointed out past the tracks.

"Much obliged, ma'am!" the Rider replied, tipping his hat. "Duck, head on over to town, see if that train brought in the mail. I'll take Miss Sweetly back to her ranch."

"Okay, Kemo-Slobby!"

"Why do you keep calling him that?" Suzannah asked as the Rider pulled her onto the horse behind him.

The Rider's chest swelled with pride. "It means Great-Paleface-Hero."

Sitting Duck climbed onto his horse and said, "No it doesn't."

"But…but you said…"

"Me lie," the Indian confessed. "Sitting Duck is heap intuitive and empathic soul. Not have heart to tell you it mean Paleface-Loser-With-No-Friends-To-Ride-With. Me no like to hurt Rider's feelings." The Rider was flabbergasted. Before he could recover, the Indian dug his heels into his horse with a "Giddy up, Decoy!" and raced up the hills towards town.

With a heavy sigh, the Rider spurred his own horse yelling, "Hi-ho, Sterling, away!" The white horse thundered across the prairie like a shot.

"My ranch is the other way!" Suzannah cried.

Sitting Duck rode into Dehydrated Gulch and quickly found the railroad station. The postmaster was a bespectacled man with a white mustache, and the Indian found him looking through the new mail.

"Yes, I'm Squint, the postmaster," said the little man.

"What can I do fer you, young lady?"

The Indian's eyes went wide. "Me brave!" he insisted. "Sitting Duck sent to see if package come for Lonesome Rider."

Mr. Squint tapped his chin thoughtfully. "You mean a package about so big, from the A-OK Adhesive and Solvent Company of Hoboken, New Jersey, marked 'Urgent', 'Rush', and 'Fragile'?"

The Indian smiled broadly. "Yes, that sound right!"

"Sorry, ma'am, 'taint here," Squint said. "Didn't know the Rider was in town, so I told them to try at the next stop."

Sitting Duck slumped his shoulders. "Thanks, anyway. Me better ride out to the Double-Uno and tell him bad news. Can you tell me how to get there?"

Before Mr. Squint could reply, a trio of burly cowboys interrupted. "Did you say the Double-Uno Ranch?" one growled.

"Yes," said the Indian, "Have important news for Lonesome Rider. Him take woman back to ranch."

The three cowboys gasped. One gulped and drawled, "The Lonesome Rider? At the Double-Uno!" Another mumbled, "The boss won't like this!"

"Don't worry about this, pops," the first cowboy told the postmaster. "We'll help him out. Come with us, friend." He slipped a hand around Sitting Duck's back and urged him towards the door.

"Me not know..." the Indian replied, "Sitting Duck's mother told him to not go off with big, mean-looking, ugly strangers."

"Fair enough, I can fix that," said the first cowboy. "I'm Bad Butch, this here is Horrible Hank, and that's Snakebite Cecil." The other two snarled greetings.

"Much better!" the Indian exclaimed. "Mother say nothing about going off with big, mean-looking, ugly friends! Sitting Duck feel much better now!"

"Good!" said Butch. "Come with us, we're on our way to the Double-Uno, too. We can show you a short-cut. It's right down this shadowy alley and through the banker's abandoned warehouse..."

Sterling passed through the gates, entering the ranch.

"Well, here we are, safe and sound at the Double-Oh-No," said the Rider.

"The Double-*Uno*." Suzannah corrected him. "It's about time! I've only got until five o'clock to come up with a brilliant plan to save my ranch! I'm thinking: bake sale!"

"Well it's not my fault ol' Sterling got a flat!" the Rider said defensively as he helped Suzannah dismount. "Thanks for fixing it, by the way."

She sniffed haughtily. "You're most welcome, I'm sure." She was about to turn away when it occurred to her to ask, "Why couldn't you do it?"

The Rider cleared his throat with embarrassment. "Well… the truth is… I can't. Not since that incident in Canyon Bottom."

"What happened in Canyon Bottom?" asked Suzannah.

A frown formed beneath the mask as the Rider took deep, angry breaths. "Some sneakin'… thievin'… cussin'… cattle-rustlin' DIRTY DOG…" The anger instantly evaporated from his voice, which turned weak and embarrassed. "…put glue on my saddle."

Suzannah tried to stifle a gasp with one hand over her mouth. "You poor, poor man."

"Don't you cry for me, ma'am," said the Rider, "I'm hot on his trail, and he'll get his in the end, too!" Then, with another "Hi-ho," he pulled on the reins and Sterling, that majestic charger, reared up on his hind legs as the Rider raised his white hat with one hand and waved farewell. Then horse and rider sped through the gates and across the plain, a steaming mound of stinky goo was the only evidence they left behind.

The Lonesome Rider was nearly to town when he found Decoy ambling across the dusty hills, with Sitting Duck sprawled across his back. The Rider pulled up beside him, grabbed the Indian by the shoulders and pulled him upright. The Indian was badly bruised and blood trickled from one corner of his mouth.

"Duck! Are you all right? Speak to me, Duck!"

"Oh, Kemo-Slobby!" he rasped, clutching to his friend for support. "Three bad men, they work for the banker. They beat heap-much snot out of me. They say if you do not leave lady's ranch they will do more!"

"More? Why those… those…" the Rider searched

his mind for an appropriate derogative. "Sneakin'! Theivin'! Cussin'! Cattle rustlin'! DIRTY DOGS! I'd like to SEE them try and beat more snot out of you! You say they were headed for the Widow Sweetly's ranch?" Sitting Duck, still gasping for painful breaths, nodded. "Then we'd better get over there and explain to them how I don't take kindly to threats! Let's go!"

With a kick of the Rider's heels, Sterling took off, followed by Decoy, who had no choice. The Rider had forgotten to let go of his reins.

The two rode into the Double-Uno, and saw no sign of life. Somewhere behind the big ranch house, black smoke climbed into the sky.

The Rider whistled. "She must have some serious baking going on!" he said as he tugged on the reins. "We'd better go warn her 'fore we go looking for them villains."

But the source of that smoke was not an oven; it was a fire pit by the mouth of a mine. Suzannah Sweetly was there, tied up again, in a mine cart filled with dynamite. Bad Butch, Horrible Hank, and Snakebite Cecil stood around her with their guns at the ready. A sinister man with a handlebar mustache turned and watched as they rode up beside a pair of carts parked beside the mine entrance.

"You must be the Lonesome Rider," he said as he stroked his mustache, "I heard you were here."

"You heard right," the Rider replied. "Who're you?"

"I'm J. Thaddeus Backslide, owner of the Trustworthy Bank and Trust, and you're too late, Rider!" snarled the black-coated villain. "In just ten minutes this ranch and this mine will be mine!"

"A mine, eh? What sort of mine? Gold, silver, uranium, lanolin?"

Backslide chuckled. "There's a fortune in this mine, as you can see by looking in those carts next to you."

The Rider looked, then frowned in puzzlement. "This is just dirt."

"Of course its dirt!" Backslide growled, "This is a LAND mine! I shall mine out the dirt and sell it through my dummy corporation; the Boyd, Dewey, Cheetum, and Howe Real Estate

Company. I'll sell land to Easterners who want a piece of the west, and they won't even have to leave home to get it, I'll just mail it to them!" Then he laughed maniacally.

"You fiend!" Sitting Duck gasped, "You will sell land right out from under us!"

"Not if I have anything to say about it!" exclaimed the Rider, drawing his gun. Bad Butch, Horrible Hank, and Snakebite Cecil all aimed at him. The Rider tried to laugh, but couldn't so he holstered his gun. "And I guess I don't have anything to say about it."

"Well, me have heap much to say!" Sitting Duck exclaimed as he drew his bow. He pulled three arrows from the quiver and notched them all at once. He pulled the string and fired perfectly, knocking the guns from the hands of all three lackeys.

The Rider's gun was drawn again instantly. "Nice shootin', Duck. Get Miss Sweetly out of the cart."

"Okay, Kemo-Slobby," said Sitting Duck as Decoy walked slowly over to the mine cart, and the three ruffians backed away. Sitting Duck slipped off his horse and stood on the dynamite. "Not worry, we take you away from all this," he said as he picked her up under the arms.

"Oh no you won't!" Bad Butch yelled as he slapped Decoy's rump.

The horse turned on him and brayed, "Don't get fresh with me, ya perv!" Decoy slapped him across the face with a hoof, horseshoe and all. Bad Butch spun around once, then fell against the dynamite-filled mine cart, causing it to start rolling along its tracks. Sitting Duck lost his balance and dropped Suzannah onto the ground before the cart vanished into the dark mine.

Horrible Hank dove for his gun, but the Rider was too fast. His bullet dug into the ground by Hank's gun, and the ruffian jumped back, lost his balance and scrambled for anything to stop his fall. All that his hand found was Decoy's tail. Horrible Hank fell to the ground and pulled the horse's rump down upon him. The horse was about to stand up when he caught the alluring aroma of baked goods on Suzannah's dress. Decoy nuzzled her to confirm the smell of cake icing, and began gnawing through the ropes to get to it.

All this gave Snakebite Cecil enough time to retrieve his gun and start firing at the Lonesome Rider. Sterling bolted for a handy tree, scant but affective cover. The Rider fired endlessly back, unable to flee the scene even if he wanted to.

Suzannah crawled out from her ropes, and rushed to a table by the fire pit. She pulled a towel from her layer cake, grabbed a bowl of frosting and a spatula, and hastily iced her cake. Upon completion, she rushed up behind Snakebite Cecil and slammed the freshly-frosted dessert into his face.

"Aargh! My eyes!" he bellowed. He dropped his gun and staggered about blindly. "They told me this would happen if I didn't get myself a woman!" Still screaming, he wandered over to Decoy, who knocked him to the ground and began licking the icing from his face.

The Rider and Sterling came out from behind the tree and looked warily around. "Is that all of them?"

"All but me!" Backslide declared as he slipped behind Suzannah, producing a gun of his own, which he held up to her neck. "And you're too late! Any second now, it will be five o'clock!"

A thunderous explosion in the mine belched out a dust-storm. As the dust slowly cleared, a human figure could be seen. The figure walked closer, and the dust thinned, revealing Sitting Duck, noble savage and faithful sidekick.

He looked at the Rider, the banker, the widow, and the two scoundrels pinned by his horse. He coughed a few times, then said, "Ugh."

"How…" was all the banker managed to say.

Sitting Duck raised one open hand. "Me fine, thanks. How you?"

"No, I mean, how did you survive that blast? That mine cart was full of dynamite!" Backslide reminded him.

Sitting Duck waved his hand dismissively. "Duh! Me jump out of mine cart before end of line. Blast shake up whole mine; reveal heap-big gold deposit. Here, Sitting Duck make withdrawal to prove it." Then he held up a gold nugget as big as an apple.

The Rider checked his watch. "Hmm, it's only four fifty-seven. That means the mine still belongs to Miss Sweetly."

With an understanding nod, Sitting Duck calmly walked

up and put the nugget in the widow's hands. "Here, feel free to spend all in one place. You have heap more."

Suzannah stared at the nugget wide-eyed and open-mouthed for a moment before she recovered. She held it up to the banker. "Mr. Backslide? I do believe this will pay off the mortgage for my ranch!"

Disheartened, Backslide lowered his pistol and slowly took the nugget. "Gold!" he cried despairingly.

"Gold?" cried Bad Butch, Horrible Hank, and Snakebite Cecil. They quickly pushed the brown horse aside and got to their feet and charged for the mine.

"Wait big, mean-looking, ugly friends! It is heap dark in there!" Sitting Duck declared as he produced a red stick. "Here, you take-um this candle."

"Thanks!" Bad Butch replied as he snatched the stick from the Indian's hand. Then the three of them charged into the mine. Another, smaller explosion soon followed.

"This is terrible!" the banker moaned. "If the mine is full of gold, then it's of no use to me. Curses, foiled again, like in that aluminum scam a year ago!"

"Mr. Backslide, I knew you were coming, but you're darn lucky I already used my cake!" Suzannah yelled. "Now, you get offa my ranch, and don't you ever set foot on my property again!"

"Uh, yes ma'am," Backslide replied. He turned to go but stopped short before he could step in a pile of stinky brown goo. He carefully circled it, tried to smile at the three people staring at him. Then he straightened his coat, tossed the nugget into the air, caught it. He turned abruptly and slipped in a second steaming mound, only to land face-first in a third. He scrambled to his feet and ran away from the howls of laughter.

Sitting Duck laughed, "My people have a word for that, but me no think the editors would print it!"

"I do believe them horse cookies were better than any cake I coulda thrown at him!" Suzannah laughed. Then she turned to the Rider and Sitting Duck. "My heroes! How can I ever thank you?"

The Rider tipped his hat and said, "'Tweren't nuthin', ma'am."

"Nothing, him say!" Sitting Duck muttered as he climbed

onto his horse.

"It's what I do, ma'am," the Rider continued. "Good luck with the gold minin' and all. But if you'll excuse us, we've got a mail train to track down."

Sitting Duck nodded authoritatively. "Yes, should be on its way to Empty Well."

"Then let's go, Duck." The Rider pulled his white horse up on two legs. "Hi-ho, Sterling, away!" Then both horses charged over the desert.

Suzannah waved as they rode into the sunset, then stopped. "Empty Well is that-a-way!" she yelled after them, pointing.

OUTLAW GUNSLINGER POEM ~
Showing Crime, Punishment, and Remorse
J H Hobson

Bang!
Hang.
...............................dang.

THE SECRET
Paul Wittine

The cowboy's wide hat
keeps the rain off of his head
and his baldness hid

LONESOME AND THE WET SNAKE
originally published in Futures Magazine, June 2000.
Earl Staggs

Broad at the shoulder, slim at the hip, and tall in the saddle, Lonesome Jones rode Hellbent out of Tombstone. Hellbent wasn't his mule's original name, I should point out, but since no cowpoke worth his spurs would ever say, "Giddyup, Alice," he had renamed her.

True to her new name, Hellbent's slender legs churned

a roiling trail of dust as they left town. She seemed to know, somehow, that Lonesome rode a sad and despondent saddle that day. He and his best friend, Slim Pennypacker, had just split up. For years, they'd stood broad shoulder to broad shoulder, slim hip to slim hip, and cleaned up the wild and woolly streets of Tombstone. The job hadn't paid much but the Sanitation Department was the only outfit in town hiring at the time.

But despite their years together, Slim had suddenly announced his plans to strike out on his own. He'd decided to head up to a writer's retreat in Utah to write a legend about himself.

Lonesome was devastated. As he rode away, he recalled their last conversation.

"Are ya shore I can't ride along with ya, Slim?" he'd asked.

"Reckon not," Slim said in that slow-talking way of his. "You've been a good sidekick, Lonesome, but I'm fixin' to change my image. Figger I'll start dressin' all in black, work on my steely-eyed look, write a legend about myself and get famous. Cowpokes who make it big in legends don't have sidekicks."

"Singin' cowpokes do," Lonesome said hopefully.

Slim fixed him in a steely-eyed look that needed a lot of work. "I don't sing."

"Oh, yeah, I forgot," Lonesome lamented quietly. He knew the ways of the Olde West. Only cowpokes who dressed in black and perfected the steely-eyed look ever became famous in legends. Sidekicks just rode off into the sunset, never to be heard of. Accepting his fate with all the grit he could muster, he asked, "What're ya figgerin' on callin' your legend?"

Slim said, "I'm thinkin' of callin' it A Heated Debate at the Cozy Corral."

Lonesome scrunched his nose in deep thought for a moment. "Uh, Slim," he said, "ya reckon heated debate's got enough pepper to it? Why not make it a slambang gunfight?"

Slim pushed his black Stetson back on his head and rubbed his stubbled chin. "Hmmmm. Gunfight at the Cozy Corral. I like it. Only thing is, Cozy Corral sounds like a mite tame place for a slambang gunfight."

"Sounds OK to me," Lonesome said.

Slim squinted up at the sun, which was how cowpokes

developed their steely-eyed look. "Just OK, huh? Well, I'll have to ponder on it. I'll come up with somethin'."

"I know ya will," Lonesome said. "You're good with words. I'll never forget all them sayin's ya said to me. Ya got one more afore we split up?"

Slim grew pensive as Lonesome packed his saddle bags for him. Then he mounted the black stallion he'd named Calvin and said, "Always remember, Lonesome, ride like the wind and keep an ear to the ground."

Lonesome's eyes widened in awe. He didn't always understand Slim's sayings but he tried to remember them all. "Wow!" he exclaimed. "That's a good 'un, Slim. I'll never forget that 'un."

And with that, they had parted. Slim headed north toward Utah and Lonesome spurred Hellbent south because that's the way the wind was blowing that day. He knew that's what Slim had meant by "ride like the wind." He couldn't figure out how to ride with an ear to the ground but he knew it could come in handy someday. Slim's sayings always did.

For three months after that sorrowful day, Lonesome roamed the plains and prairies of the Olde West, alone and forlorn, taking whatever jobs he could rustle up. He poked a few cows here, strung a little barbed wire there, struggling to get by the best he could on his own.

One night, he reined up with the lights of Fort Worth glowing like a range fire on the horizon. He could have gone on into town and stayed in a hotel but he preferred the feel of sage brush under his back at night and the pittypat of prairie dog feet around him.

He built his campfire and filled his coffee pot for the next morning. "An empty pot don't never perk," Slim had once said. Lonesome remembered that one. He stretched, yawned, and lay down on his bedroll.

Within minutes, he jerked upright, his throat on fire, his eyes watering from a column of thick smoke rolling over him.

He swore out loud. "Dangit!"

He'd forgotten one of Slim's sayings. "Always bed down upwind." Quickly gathering his bedroll, he moved to the other side of the fire, settled in again, and was soon fast asleep.

Sometime later, he awoke to a faint sound nearby.

68

Something scraping against the ground. And a hissing noise.

It grew closer.

Lonesome opened his eyes and found himself staring straight into another pair of eyes. Black, unblinking slits on the head of a huge rattlesnake. It stopped moving and lay there less than a foot away, flicking its tongue at him. Its tail seemed to stretch back a mile.

Lonesome wasn't sure what was making the most noise—the rattling of that snake's tail or the chattering of his own teeth. But he knew the big snake could strike from that distance and he could soon be heading for the last roundup.

One of Slim's sayings played just beyond his recall. It was about snakes. What the heck was it? Then, the words flashed in his mind like lightning bolts in a Texas storm.

"A wet snake'll always curl to the left."

Yes! That was it.

Slow and easy, Lonesome slid his hand toward his coffee pot, filled with water, ready for his morning coffee. He snatched a good grip on the handle just as the rattler reared back to strike. Faster than he'd ever done anything in his life, Lonesome swung that pot up and over and doused the water on the snake.

Slim had been right again. As soon as the water splashed over him, the rattler curled to the left and kept curling until it was wound up tighter than a new boot. That snake was so wound up, all it could do was wriggle inside a pile of itself and hiss obscenities.

Lonesome breathed a sigh of relief as he watched the big rattler roll away like a lopsided soccer ball.

Then he grinned all over himself. He knew what had just happened between him and that snake on that dark starry night on that tiny patch of prairie would be told and retold from generation to generation. He knew for sure it would become a genuine legend of the Olde West. He had ridden into sunset after sunset, expecting to fade away like a cactus shadow at dawn, never to be heard of, but now he had his own legend. He would be famous. Like Slim. He envisioned riding with Slim again, traveling the legend circuit together side by side. He could even ask his old friend why wet snakes curl to the left like that.

But it was not to be.

Oh, it worked out fine for Lonesome. He lived a long

and happy life after that night, moseying from town to town, telling his legend and being famous, but he never saw Slim Pennypacker again. He once heard, though, that Slim changed his name to Wyatt something-or-other and was still working on a name for his legend about a gunfight at the Cozy Corral.

But as they say out here in the Olde West, that's a whole 'nuther story.

On Guns and Dreams and Celestial Bodies
John Weagly

Shadow Sly aimed his gun at the sky
To shoot to the ground a star

He aimed and shot, but hit he could not,
For his bullets couldn't fly that far

So Shadow Sly was a failure it seems
If you judge by his project's success

But if a cowboy's dreams are in the extremes,
Then that cowboy deserves to impress

Howlin' at the Moon
Will Morton

At night when we set round the fire,
Ol' Murphy brings out his guitar,
An' our whole singin' crew
Raise such hullabaloo
All the coyot's is deef near an' far.

Moira and Sven the Swede
Kaysee Renee Robichaud

Sweet-natured Moira fell in love with Sven the Swede because of how darned cute he looked when he did his prairie dog imitation. Those grand, blue eyes got wide as soup bowls,

70

his mouth pinched tight as a banker's purse strings, his hands curled before his chest, his knees bent and straightened, bouncing him in place like the proverbial critter. . . There was something blessed adorable about the man.

That Sven could only speak three words of English—not a one of them was repeatable in polite company—mattered little to Moira, for her heart swelled, her spirit swooned, and air fled her lungs whenever she caught sight, sound or wind of that handsome, blonde haired feller doing his prairie dog.

That he loved her too, was obvious. When he wasn't prairie dogging, Sven would mash his hat between his ham hock hands, or smile and tug on his white blonde hair, or whisper sweet sounding syllables that made not a lick of sense. She obliged him by smiling and giggling and clasping her hands while twirling at the waist, all the while wondering at the strength in his massive arms and broad shoulders, at the proud heart pounding in his chest, and the promise of what was to come on their night of wedded bliss.

Moira had a hard time convincing Father to allow a "ferner" like Sven to woo her, but Ma saw the truth. Ma saw the necessity of a love match, saw the pleasure her lovely daughter took in Sven's company, and saw just how far away any better suitors to her daughter's affections lived. Seeing all this, Ma made her choice to keep her favorite daughter as close as possible. Between the both of them, Father was outmatched.

The language barrier proved not to be insurmountable. They spoke with glances and occasional touches (All proper! Well, in so far as whenever anyone who could see were nearby they remained proper.) and their affection only increased with every passing day.

When she was sad, she had only to bat her eyelashes and there was the wide-eyed, pinched mouth bounce. Father joked that he ought to take a scattergun to the boy's head—a fit enough punishment for any *other* prairie dog—but as time passed, he grew to like having a strong lad to help around the farm. Made having no sons somehow more tolerable.

Finally, the young lovers found themselves before a preacher. When it came time to kiss the bride, the Swede did not understand and so remained curious, head cocked and frozen like winter earth. When that hesitation threatened to ruin the moment and Moira's eyes teared up, he bounced for her, and she giggled, and his arms came around her, and their lips met (for the first time in public), and his kiss was sweeter than ever, and his embrace was strong and comforting and eternal.

That night, when they were alone, the bed turned down, he lying over her, Moira felt just tight with nervousness. Here he was, her husband, atop her, his virgin bride. Her flesh got all goosepimply, her breathing got uneven, and her terror was plain.

Then, that look came into his eyes. She giggled, as he prairie dogged, and the icy nervousness melted in an instant. He bobbed against her a spell, and she realized what a catch she had. She winced at first, and then she moaned beneath him, and then, when he was done, she sighed.

Poor little prairie dogs. Cute critters, pests according to Father, but they were ultimately small enough that they didn't cause too much harm. Strange to think that a lout as big and broad as the Swede Sven should be likewise.

They lay together a while, until he fell to snoring like a hog, and she patted his back, feeling the swell of heart, the swoon of spirit, and. . .

Shouldn't there have been something else?

Something magical?

Maybe tomorrow. Or the day after. Or next week. Year. Decade.

Moira hugged her man, and he mumbled something between snores, and she didn't care what it was he said because it sounded so. . . So sweet. So loving.

No Fights Without Bets
Alex Moisi

Jack Colt was a self-made man, the kind of guy who upon hearing of a gold rush would make sure to arrive there within a day so he could sell shovels at twice their price. He was also the only one who had dared to buy the Old Coyote bar in Deathwood, the only town on the West Coast to have more gunfights than residents.

Normally, the daily shootings and the drunken crowd of rowdy cowboys would have driven a regular pub out of business, and a regular pub owner into the loony bin, or at the very least the poor house. After all there are only so many chairs, broken over someone's head that a man can replace. But Jack had an eye for business. The first thing he did, after purchasing the place was to add a bookie to the bar. He then changed the dusty sign proclaiming "NO FIGHTS" to "NO FIGHTS without bets." Soon, the Old Coyote bar was making enough money from gambling that Jack could even hire a man insane enough to risk his life playing the piano in that mad joint. Times were good.

However, no matter how much money he made and how many people congratulated him for putting Deathwood on the map, Jack was still careful. After all, the usual crowd in his bar was made up of gunfighters and ruffians, and you always had to be on your toes around that kind of pleasant company. Luckily for Jack, in addition to an eye for business he also had a nose for trouble; he could smell it a mile away and be gone by the time trouble came around, looking for him. And that Friday evening, as *the stranger* entered his bar, Jack's nostrils suddenly widened to worrisome circumferences.

It wasn't that the stranger was particularly fearsome-looking; on the contrary, he was rather short and skinny, and he was dressed in the loose clothes that the Chinamen usually wore. Even more, there wasn't a single hair on the stranger's head or face; he was as smooth as a baby. It was hard to look menacing when you resembled a toddler's buttocks. But even so, there was something about the stranger that made Jack stop from wiping a dirty glass with a dirtier piece of cloth and look up.

"Hello," the stranger said with a very thick Asian accent. "I'm looking for Bill The Gun."

Following one of the many unwritten rules of the universe, the bar went dead quiet and everyone turned towards the stranger. A jarring, off-key note came from the direction of the piano as the piano-man crawled into a small hiding hole carved into the side of his instrument. He might have been mad enough to play in the most dangerous bar on the West Coast, but he knew when it was time to hide.

"I'm Chen," the stranger offered "and I was told Bill likes to drink here. I hope I was not misinformed."

This time, a tall man who resembled a bear slowly rose from his chair. Bill "The Gun" Bronco was the current champion of the Old Coyote betting club, having won gunfights, fistfights, knife-fights and drink-till-the-first-one-passes-out-fights against anyone who dared challenge him. Some said he once killed a man with his bare hands, others claimed he first ripped off the man's hands and then killed him with them. Either way, he was not the kind of guy you came looking for.

"Whatcha want?" Bill asked, launching a glob of chewing tobacco across the room. His aim was perfect, not one drop missing the spit bucket. A short lived murmur of appreciation circled the room.

"You borrowed money last month from Mama Jo," Chen interrupted the moment. "Two hundred twenty five dollars that needs to be returned."

Bill chuckled to himself for a second before responding.

"It don't quite work that way. I took money from a lot of folk last month but I didn't borrow nothing. I pointed a gun and I took it, forever. There's nothing to return. So, you tell this Mama, to forget it."

Chen smiled and took a few small steps into the bar.

"I'm afraid that's not possible. You don't owe Mama Jo the money anymore. She sold the debt to Mr. Ka who sold it to Mr. Li who hired me to retrieve the money and the interest."

The silence deepened to a point where you could hear the rust flaking off rarely used mental cogwheels. It was at this point that Jack, despite his better judgment, decided to intervene. The truth was he felt bad for the poor stranger who was about to become dog food, if the dogs could chew around all the lead that was soon going to fill his body.

"Hey, mister," Jack called towards Chen. "Come over here and have a drink on the house. I'm sure we can talk this over like civilized people. You don't want to go around picking fights with fine gentlemen, do you?"

"What you sayin'?" Bill grunted, his tone suddenly serious. "You say this little man wants to fight me? You think he can fight me?"

"No," Jack hurried.

"Yes," Chen smiled.

Normally, at this point Bill would have picked up a table and crashed it into the other man's head until one or the other broke. But this was the Old Coyote bar, and there was a big sign proclaiming: "NO FIGHTS without bets." So Bill jabbed the

Asian man with a long, hairy finger and grumbled something about the town not being big enough for two men, so Bill would kill both and then ride away in the sunset, or something like that.

All in all, the fight was delayed only as long as it took for the men present to furiously place their bets against Chen. The odds were bad, 50 to 1 against the stranger, but since it was a sure win for Bill everybody put some money on the fight. Jack wrote the bets down without really paying attention; his eyes kept darting towards Chen who was sitting in a corner smiling patiently and listening to Bill's confused insults. It must have been the same trusting smile the dodo birds had as they watched the first colonists hunt them. The stranger didn't even seem to have a gun.

Within an hour both fighters were in position outside the bar, on Main Street. The sun was setting and long shadows crept around, but a little darkness never stopped determined and slightly inebriated men from shooting guns at each other. So Jack read the brief rules that amounted to "The first one dead loses" and wished both of the men good luck.

"So, buddy," Bill grinned as the two of them faced each other. "Didn't think today was your funeral, eh?"

The stranger opened his mouth to respond but Bill was faster. Before any words could come out, his gun was drawn and aiming. By the time Chen said "Well," the first bullet was shot, aiming to kill. The rest of the chamber followed in quick, calculated bursts and with each BANG! Bill's grin widened more and more.

What exactly happened next remained a matter of great debate among those who saw the fight. Some said that Chen was a demon of sorts while others claimed that he had to be one of a team of ten men that all looked identical. One thing was certain: he couldn't have been a normal man. As Bill shot at him, so fast his own shadow was struggling to keep up, Chen jumped, twisted, somersaulted and slid, avoiding each single one of the bullets and drawing closer to the other man with every step. The last few feet he simply flew through the evening air, hitting the large man's chest. Bill collapsed with a surprised expression and no heartbeat. All it had taken was one kick and the Old Coyote bar champion was dead.

Silence fell over Main Street. Everyone there had seen

countless fights of every kind, but no one had seen someone move like that. The first one to regain his wits and slowly slink away was the piano-man. He left town that very day, pushing his piano in front of him and swearing never to return to that cursed place again. The tips were great but you had to draw the line somewhere.

"I think this entitles me to some money," Chen said, presenting Jack with a ticket stub for a bet.

Jack, his jaw still slack, read the number on the ticket. His business instinct took over from a very confused bartender, and did a quick calculation. The stranger, of course, had placed a bet on himself, a bet worth just ten dollars but with odds of 50 to 1 that amounted to five hundred dollars. The thought that he shouldn't pay crossed Jack's mind for just a second before he remembered how much he enjoyed being alive. The cash, in a bag very appropriately marked with a $ symbol, quickly exchanged hands.

"Thank you," Chen said, bowing.

No one dared move as the small man started on his way, towards the town's northern exit.

"Wait," Jack called, his mind still reeling with the loss of five hundred dollars. "I could use a man like you around my bar. I can give you a job."

"I already have a job," Chen smiled. "I'm a collection agent," he said before walking into the sunset.

No Poker?
Will Morton

Th' saloon where we go when we're paid,
Is run by this feller Kincaid.
"If yer wanna play cards,"
He says to my pards,
"We got Crazy Eights, Fish, and Old Maid!"

WILD AND WESTERN LIMERICKS
Rob Mancebo

There was a tall waddie named Hunk
who let loose some bad air in his bunk
Soon the 'cowboy hotel'
was rife with the smell
like someone had skinned-out a skunk.

There was a bull-whacker named Bill
who hauled freight up a mighty steep hill
he whipped and he cursed
gave the team all his worst
Till they lunged and they pulled with a will.

There was a blonde cowgirl name Dot
who wore a low belt-gun and shot:
Seven wolves and two hares
an assortment of bears
and a fellow who snored in his cot.

There was a plump cowgirl named Marge
whose seat was spectacularly large
she dated young Ollie
who was clever and jolly
And made her a chair from a barge.

There was a horse-breaker named Sly
who gave that bronc 'Devil' a try
he hung on while it bucked
till he ran out of luck
then that cowpoke, he learned how to fly.

There once was a cowgirl named Rose
who got young Jim to propose
Jimmy made her his spouse
to take care of his house
now she's got a bull ring through his nose.

There was an old rooster next door
who crowed every morning at four
he thought it was fun
till Pa got out his gun
now he don't do it no more.

We're Such an Unfortunate Family
Lyn McConchie

We're such an unfortunate family. Back when stages first started in the region one of my great uncles drove a stage—very briefly. About his seventh day on the job he had steadied the stage-horses for the long run up the hill before town when a man riding one horse and leading a saddled mount without a rider pulled up behind him. The spare mount moved up to one side of the stage, the rider swung his horse right up to the door on the other side, and before my great uncle could ask what was going on, it all began.

The rider leaned down, opened the door, jumped into the stage, crawled across the three passengers, swung out of the other door and leapt astride his spare mount. He called to the first horse and it galloped ahead to join him. My great uncle Mathew was annoyed. This man was a flashy-looking chap, with a brocade waistcoat, slicked down hair, and a fancy suit with the pant's bottoms tucked into short boots, and my great uncle disliked the look of him. Besides, two of the passengers were respectable ladies and they were complaining, and he felt that all of this was quite irregular. So he called out to the man who was about to ride away off to his right.

"Say, stranger, what was all that about?"

In a very fancy accent, the dude called back. "Nothing at all, mister, I'm an actor and it's just a stage I'm going through." Then he started laughing like a fool. Well, my great uncle didn't like that, so he up and shot the man, and once he got back to the depot, he resigned. He said to the manager that he had better things to do with his time that to provide a stage for bad actors.

We're such an unfortunate family. My great uncle did eventually marry. She was a pleasant woman who came of quite a good family. She died soon after her son was born and my great uncle who'd come to the conclusion that civilization was a snare and a delusion moved right back into the mountains to an isolated basin to live with the boy.

He raised him alone, never letting him come into town or meet anyone else. The land my great uncle owned was pretty large in area, almost twenty thousand acres and James, the boy, became an excellent rancher, always concerned for his stock and taking care that they were never ill-treated. But when he turned twenty-one my great uncle had a problem. He wanted James to inherit the ranch, and to do that he needed to take him into town to sign papers acknowledging that they were father and son and that James would be his heir.

Great Uncle Mathew worried for weeks over this. A town could be a corrupting influence and he'd spent twenty-one years making sure that James was innocent about the wickedness of the world. But it had to be done so he sneaked them into the town before first light, spent the day in the lawyer's office — having told the man that if they could stay there unseen he'd double his fee — and meanwhile they signed all the necessary papers.

Just before dark, Great Uncle Mathew went out to get the wagon, brought it around to the back door of the lawyer's office, got James into it and started for home. They were just driving past the new schoolhouse a little out of town when the door opened and a young woman came walking out of the building and down the road right by the wagon.

James stared at her and she slowed and stared back. I have to admit that having seen the photos of James as a young man he was astonishingly handsome. James turned to his father.

"What odd clothing that young man is wearing."

"That is a woman, son. You've read about them in the bible, and now you've seen one we can go on home."

But it was too late. James was captured. "Father, if that's a woman, I want one."

"No, no, son, women are a snare and a delusion, you don't want to have anything to do with them."

"But father, I do. Please, get her for me. Persuade her to return with us."

Great Uncle Mathew sighed. It'd all end badly, he was convinced, but if James had set his heart on this young woman, it could have been worse. She was modestly dressed, obviously educated, and he believed that she wouldn't have any relatives to pester them, or she wouldn't have been working. So he dismounted from the wagon and called to the girl who halted to listen.

It took some talking but James was very good-looking,

Mathew explained how much land they had, and offered to build a whole extra set of rooms for them after the honeymoon and in the end she agreed. James wanted her to come with them right there and then, they found the minister, and by ten o'clock James and Miss Mason were married and on their way back to the ranch in the mountains.

Great Uncle Mathew put a pack on his horse once they arrived, saddled his mount, and stepped into the saddle.

"A man should be alone with his wife for a while, son. I'll take a swing around the boundary to check everything is all right out there. I'll be gone for a couple of weeks. You take good care of your wife, do right by her, and be kind to her."

"I will, father."

Great Uncle Mathew was gone for that two weeks and by the time he headed for home he was looking forward to his daughter-in-law's cooking and a seat by the fire with some good conversation. His horse walks into the corral and James comes out to meet his father but there's no sign of the girl.

"Hello father, it's good to see you back."

"It's good to be back, son, now, where's that pretty little wife of yours?"

James looks sad, "I guess we won't talk about her, father."

Great Uncle Mathew is horrified; surely the girl can't have gotten sick of marriage this soon? "Why," he asks. "Where is she?"

James gives this long sad sigh. "It was like this, father; two days ago she went down to the corral to saddle up for a ride. Her horse got excited, he was swinging around while she held the reins and she lost her balance, she slipped and fell and her leg was broken."

"What, the poor child. So where is she now?"

James points towards the back of the ranch house. "Why, father, I had to shoot her."

THE TRAGIC TALE OF TYRANNOSAURUS TEX
Matthew Baugh

When it comes to the great sauropod gunmen of the west, there are a few names that stand out. There's Kid Gwangi, of course, and the Deinonychus they called *La Garra Terrible* but there's no doubt that the greatest of all was the big lizard known as Tyrannosaurus Tex.

He had a reputation as the worst killer west of the Pecos, and the law didn't seem to be able to do much about it. That was what brought Ezekiel Blackwood into Sheriff Crawford's office that morning.

"Sheriff," he said. "That Tyrannosaurus Tex is walking around town as bold as you please. I demand you put him in jail."

"Now Zeke," the Sheriff replied, "you know there's a practical problem with that. There's no jail as can hold him."

"If he tries to escape—"

"That ain't what I mean," the Sheriff interrupted. "Tex measures forty-nine feet from nose to tail. There's no jail *large enough* to hold him. 'Sides, I got no charges against him in this jurisdiction."

"What do you mean?" Zeke said. "Everyone knows that he robbed the overland stage."

"Now, Zeke, if I knew that for sure I'd arrest him, but the witnesses said the robber wore a bandana over his face."

"He also ate two passengers and one of the horses!" Zeke said. "Who else but Tex would do something like that?"

"Well, maybe it was a dinosaur," the Sheriff admitted, "but that don't mean it was Tex. It could have been Stegosaurus Pete, for example."

"Sheriff, you know Pete ain't a real dinosaur," Zeke said. "He's just such a pea-brain that people call him that."

"I'm sorry, son," the Sheriff replied. "Without better evidence there's nothing I can do."

"It burns me up to see him wandering around as free as a bird," Zeke said.

"It's actually kinda appropriate," the Sheriff said. "From what Miss Laura says, birds are the evolutionary descendants of dinosaurs."

"Maybe I'll just have to take matters into my own hands," Zeke said.

"I wouldn't recommend it," the Sheriff replied. "It ain't a good idea to mess with five tons of angry lizard, not when he's packing iron.

Danged coward! Zeke thought as he stomped down the street. *He knows that Tex is guilty as sin; he's just scared to face up to him.*

It frustrated him that no one in town seemed willing to admit how dangerous Tex was; not the sheriff, and not even Miss Laura.

Truth be told, it was Laura's interest in the carnivorous outlaw that bothered him the most. He'd been sweet on the school-marm since she'd moved to Raptor's Gulch the previous year, but her first love was paleontology. When Tex had taken an interest in her, Zeke found it unbearable.

"I'm sorry, Zeke," she had said yesterday afternoon. "Ordinarily I'd love to see you, but Tex and I have plans."

"You're letting that lizard take you to dinner?"

"Not exactly, but he left a bison carcass on my doorstep this morning. It's such a manly gesture of affection."

"How can you think of seeing him?" Zeke asked. "Don't you know that he's a cold-blooded killer?"

"That's a common misconception," she replied. "Actually, dinosaurs are endothermic."

The look in her eyes had settled it as far as Zeke was concerned. Tyrannosaurus Tex *had* to go!

He made his way to the general store, hoping his special order had arrived.

"Yessir!" Cletus Swenson said as he placed the crate on the counter. "Special order from Colt Firearms." He whistled in awe as he removed the massive rifle and handed it to Zeke.

"What is it?"

"It's a .50 caliber buffalo gun," Zeke replied. "Except this one has a Winchester-style repeating action."

"So you can fire off a lot of powerful rounds real fast? Sounds impressive, but what..." The shopkeeper's face grew

pale as the implication hit him. "You can't be planning what I'm thinking of, can you?"

"You know what they say, Zeke replied. "God made all men — and dinosaurs — but it was Colonel Colt that made them equal."

He smiled grimly as he took the rifle and left.

When Tyrannosaurus Tex strode into town that afternoon, Zeke was waiting for him.

He probably shouldn't wear the hat, Zeke thought. In fact, the ten-gallon Stetson on Tex's eight foot long skull looked about nine-hundred and ninety gallons too small.

Holding the rifle low, Zeke stepped into the center of the street.

"Tyrannosaurus Tex!" he shouted, "I'm callin' you out!"

The dinosaur paused.

Probably the first time anyone's ever challenged him like this, Zeke thought. He felt as if his innards, questioning his sanity, were trying to jump ship and flee. He forced himself to breathe slowly and steadily. After a moment he was able to speak again.

"Slap leather, lizard!"

Tex reached for one of the .45 Colt Peacemakers he always wore as Zeke raised his rifle and fired. The big slug made a small hole in the dinosaur's massive chest. Two more shots put two more holes near the first. Tex wasn't down but he was hurting.

Why hasn't he fired back? Zeke thought. Then he realized that the tyrannosaur's puny forearms were too short to reach his holsters.

"You big fake!" He shouted. "You never were a gunfighter!"

Tex let out a terrible roar and charged with gaping jaws. Zeke nearly panicked then, but managed to fire three more shots. Just before the badly-wounded tyrannosaur reached his target, he collapsed.

"You had enough?" Zeke said.

Tex didn't answer, but painfully rose to his feet, growling his defiance. Zeke watched him for a moment, amazed at the behemoth's determination.

"Here," he said, taking out his own pistol and tossing it to the dinosaur. "I ain't shooting an unarmed opponent."

Tex caught the weapon and fumbled with it for several moments.

"Aw, for pity's sake!" Zeke said. "Didn't you ever realize that you can't use a single action revolver unless you've got thumbs to cock it?"

With a dejected snort the big reptile let the weapon fall to the dusty street and limped out of town.

They made a hero out of Zeke, though Miss Laura wasn't so keen on him.

"Did you think I'd be impressed with the way you bullied poor Tex?" she demanded.

"Bullied?" Zeke stammered. "Miss Laura, he's fifty times as big as me."

"You're so smug, you and your opposable thumbs," she said. Then she rode out of town in her buggy, hoping to find her injured beau.

Zeke stared after her for a long time. He hadn't thought that evolution was supposed to work like that.

They made Zeke the sheriff. He eventually married a dance hall girl who was interested in paleobotany, but he never forgot Miss Laura.

And what became of Tyrannosaurus Tex and his schoolteacher sweetheart? Some say they went to Bolivia and robbed trains. Others claim they went to Washington where she got a job as a docent at the Smithsonian and he found work as an exhibit. No one really knows for sure, but that's the way it is with legends.

THE TIME MACHINE
Alex Moisi

Greg Holster was a simple, practical man. He greeted the passengers, if there were any, loaded the mail sacks, and got his coach from point A to point B. Most of the time that was it: no excitement, no worries. He'd take a day off, then load up and start all over again. It was the perfect job, there was nothing better than watching the flat, desert plains fly by and occasionally cry out: "Giddy-Up!" so that his four horses wouldn't get too bored. Then again, there were those moments when Greg sighed and wondered why he hadn't become a cantaloupe farmer like his dad.

This was definitely such a moment, and the narrow valley where Greg's coach was stopped echoed with his sighs. About ten feet in front of the horses, someone had built a complicated and shiny contraption that was puffing a very thick cloud of steam.

"Don't move!" came the usual call as Greg sighed again. "This is a hold-up," the rather thin voice continued as Greg mouthed the words along with it.

"So what do you plan to steal?" the coach driver asked in a bored voice. "The mail sacks? My lunch?"

There was a brief pause as the robber made his way from behind the puffing contraption, holding what looked to Greg like the most ancient shotgun in the world. However, that wasn't the only peculiar thing about the robber. Instead of the stereotypical handkerchief-over-the-nose technique, the tall and skinny man in front of Greg had chosen to wear a pair of dark goggles and a train conductor's hat.

"Nice disguise," Greg said politely. "Very original. The road block, too — they usually just put some logs in the way instead of a steaming…machine…thing."

"Get away from the coach," the robber demanded, shaking his gun.

"Also, they have more threatening weapons," Greg continued, unperturbed. "You think you can shoot that thing faster than I can roll to the side and draw my Colt? I'm a good aim and that thing looks like it needs a few minutes to warm up."

The robber seemed to consider this for a second, but shook his head.

"I need your horses. That *machine-thing,* as you called it, is the very first steam-powered time machine in the world, and your horses are going to be the first living animals to travel through time."

Greg had been robbed many times — or rather, robbers had tried to mug Greg many times — but this was definitely a new twist.

"You see, it's all rather easy," the robber offered, probably because of Greg's confused face. "It's all about how fast something travels. If you can shoot a bullet fast enough that it catches up to time itself, you basically have a time-travelling bullet that will fire into the future."

"Sounds like a lot of work just to get a gun."

"No, no, no," the robber cried, waving his hands emphatically. "It's not a gun, not at all, you're missing the point. This is an exponential engine. It can double the speed of an object every few minutes if the object enters the machine with a constant velocity. If these horses, for example, were to enter through the left side, running at full speed, their velocity will increase a thousandfold by the time they are catapulted outside on the other side, in another time."

"You want to shoot my horses out of a cannon?" Greg asked harshly, his hand twitching towards his gun holster and his eyes narrowing. He was finally starting to understand what the stranger had built and he didn't like it in the least.

"Oh, it's not that simple. Quite complex science went into building the motor behind it, and it takes a tremendous amount of energy to give the impulses necessary for the exponential increases. Unfortunately, most of my money went into building the machine and keeping it running—coal is terribly expensive nowadays. This, of course, means that finding funds for experimental subjects is rather complicated, hence this whole robbery deal. A tad bit embarrassing, but it's all in the pursuit of Truth, with a capital T."

"You want to shoot my horses out of a steam powered cannon?" Greg's voice became harsher and his eyes narrowed further until they resembled a thin line.

"I said it's not that simple," the robber repeated, oblivious to the imminent danger. "There are many unknown variables. For all I know, the whole thing could misfire terribly, but in the name of science we must move forward no matter what the risks, no matter what costs, in order to find Truth with a capital T—"

Greg snapped before the robber could finish his speech. He was a simple man who spent a lot of time around his horses and liked them a lot better than all the steam motors in the world. He was also a practical man; one well placed bullet twisted the engine's exhaust pipe out of shape. By the time the robber had realized what was going on, Greg had covered his ears, and the time machine had exploded, flying into the sky.

"Well," Greg said after the steam cleared off. "I reckon the road is clear again and your machine is approaching the speed of time. I do hope I helped clear up some confusions about unknown variables. Now, if you'd be so kind, I have two sacks of letters that need to be delivered."

With a loud "Giddy-Up!" Greg was back on his way. Behind him a very confused robber stood wide-eyed, staring at his life's work as it hurtled through the air.

THE SANITY OF HATS
John Weagly

A cowboy's hat is a special thing
Whether ten-gallon or twenty-two quarts

Without it he feels under-dressed
And his day will be all out of sorts

It keeps off the rain and the sun beating down
It can fan a fire or water a horse

And in regards to high plains fashion
A hat is a requirement, of course

So every day remember your lid
Or your "Conk-Cover," if so inclined

For without that wrapper up on his head
A cowboy could plumb lose his mind!

GUNPLAY AND HAIKU IN BELCHING GULCH
Aaron Polson

A stranger rode into Belching Gulch with his wind-up minstrel on a burro at his side. A tall man, he tethered his horse outside of Lucky Jim's Good Times Saloon, did the same for the burro, and gave his little buddy a few hearty cranks before the two strode into the bar. The trail had been hot that day, and the stranger had a hankering for a tall sarsaparilla. The wind-up, a sort of metal-man made of bits of tin, brass, and spare watch parts, just wanted some shade.

Upon entering the saloon, the clanking companion sputtered for a moment before opening his metal jaws.

"The trail was so hot.
Made of metal and small cogs,
I prefer the shade."

The piano man stopped, and in the silence, all eyes in the place swiveled to drink in the tall man and his metal companion. Four poker players rubbed their stubbly chins in unison. The bartender pulled at his moustache. In the far corner of the room, a lone man sat in shadows with half a bottle of whiskey on his table. He leaned forward when the wind-up spoke.

"What'll ya have, mister?" the bartender asked as the stranger approached.

"Root beer. Make it frosty. We have a ways to go yet. My name's Weedly, by the way. Dirk Weedly." He paused, perhaps waiting for the sound of thunder or a gasp from the piano man. "We're headed for Dodge City — it much farther?"

The poker players chuckled quietly. The man in the corner poured himself another glass.

"Depends on which way you going, east or west?"

Dirk nodded to the barkeep. "Heading west."

"Then you done passed it up 'bout ten miles back." The bartender pushed a tall mug of root beer in front of Dirk.

"Oh heck," Dirk muttered, his face blossoming red.

The metal man started again:

"Hell, dreams of fire,

90

A place forever burning
And not very nice."

The bartender steadied his hands on his hips. "What do you call that contraption?"

Dirk smiled away his embarrassment and patted the tin-can head of the thing. "Oh, my sidekick? His name's Yoshi."

"What's he sayin'?"

"Oh...that. He calls it 'high-coo'." He pulled at his gun belt. "I won him in a game of chance back in San Francisco from a Japanese shop owner." Dirk pulled the root-beer mug to his mouth.

"He for sale?" a cold voice said from behind Dirk.

Dirk spun to see the dark man from the corner standing behind him. The light revealed a criss-cross of scars painted across the man's face. The dark man rested one hand on the pearl handle of his pistol grip.

"My name's John. John Carney. I work for the carnival that's stopping through here on our way out to Denver." His hand tightened on the pistol grip. "We sure could use an oddity like that in the show. Draw lots of folks."

"Sorry," Dirk started. "Not interested in selling."

"Well then..." Carney stepped closer to Dirk, his spurs rattling at his ankles. "How's about another game?"

The poker players stopped and two of them stood. All eyes were on Dirk Weedly. He tugged at his shirt collar, suddenly too hot in the dusty saloon. John Carney narrowed his dark eyes. "What's it going to be?"

Yoshi piped up with another poem:

"A challenged refused
Can lead to lost dignity
And the name coward."

Dirk coughed as he tapped the wind-up with his boot. "I guess I'm in. What'll it be? Poker? Blackjack? I don't plan on losing, Mr. Carney."

Carney pointed at Dirk's gun belt. "I was thinking a little challenge worthy of a gunslinger. You fancy yourself a gunslinger, Weedly?"

Unable to back away from the challenge without losing

face, Dirk Weedly found himself standing in the alleyway behind Lucky Jim's. The metal man was at his side, whirring and clicking away, while the rest of the saloon-goers and about half the town (another four people) looked on.

"Here's the challenge fella. I've set up them bottles up at the end of this here alleyway." Carney waved in the distance with his pistol. "I'll take my shot first. If you can break as many, or more 'n me, you win."

Dirk glanced about, drinking in the eager faces of the townspeople. Belching Gulch was a quiet burg, and such excitement had been a long time coming. He rubbed his neck, looked down at Yoshi's metal face, and nodded. "Sure. Sounds good."

John Carney stepped to the middle of the alley, leveled his revolver and cracked six shots in quick succession. One, two, three, four, five bottles shattered, leaving the six unscathed. He twirled the spent revolver on his finger and dropped it in the holster at his hip.

Another poem from the metal minstrel:

"Carney's aim was true
You can't shoot as well as he
I will miss you, Dirk."

Dirk Weedly was outmatched; he knew it, and the beads of sweat rolling down his forehead broadcast that fact to the folks standing around that dusty alley. He was outmatched, but not outsmarted. With one hand he thumped Yoshi's tin shoulder while the other drew his pistol from its holster.

"I'm going to miss you, too."

Dirk Weedly stepped into the center of the alley. The place was quiet save for the sound of dry prairie wind brushing past the back of the saloon. Dirk wiped away the sweat from his forehead and squinted at the fresh bottles that Carney placed. Six of them. The crowd pressed in, the silence becoming thick with their anxious breath. Dirk didn't like to lose.

He raised his pistol, steadied the barrel, and took aim at the first of the bottles. His other hand dropped to his side where it clenched into a white knuckled fist. He squinted, but the bottles seemed to dance. His gun-hand began to shake.

"Go on, stranger," the bartender prodded, eager to file

the onlookers back into his saloon for more drinks.

Dirk inhaled, sucking in a good lungful of cool breeze. His finger pulled gently at the trigger. The crowd pressed in even more.

Yoshi broke the silence:

> *"Your cowardice grows*
> *every passing moment*
> *don't be a chicken."*

Dirk wheeled, pointed the gun at the wind-up minstrel, and fired six quick shots into its head and chest. The wind-up lurched forward, opened and shut its clanking mouth, and fell lifeless on the packed dirt.

"You win, Mr. Carney." Dirk slipped his gun in its holster and strode through the back door of the saloon and out the front, climbed onto his mud brown horse and rode back into the east, two hours too early for the sunset and going the wrong way besides.

SID THE SHERIFF
Jax

There once was a sheriff called Sid,
Who looked just like Billy the Kid,
He lived on canned beans,
But that blew up his jeans,
And then he just flipped his lid.

COW-JINKS
Will Morton

Them critters was smart, I could tell,
But I wouldn't of thought they could spell,
Till a yearling complained,
"This here ranch's name
Is Tilt Seven, not no Lazy L!"

Thieving Varmints

Adrienne Lockhart

Yager had taken to sitting outside and staring at the open prairie for hours, sometimes even days. Two years previously he had made the dangerous haul out West in the hopes of remaking himself into a rough and tumble cowboy. He hadn't even taken a wagon. His meager possessions and supplies fit solidly on the back of a sturdy moth-ridden donkey by the name of Bean. Yager had wanted to purchase a midnight black stallion with blazing red eyes to start what he envisioned as a powerful transformation from poor beggar to great folk hero, but he could only afford Bean with his pitiful stash.

Bean had born him slowly to a remote dale far off any beaten path. Yager, though he daily cursed the beast, silently admitted time and again that he probably shouldn't have drank an entire flask of blindingly powerful moonshine and then collapsed in a drunken stupor atop the boney back of Bean. By the time he had awakened, sore and with a raging migraine, he and Bean were hopelessly lost. There was naught to do except set up shop. Now he sat as he did each morning outside of a ramshackle lean-to with a shoddily crafted earthen mug of bitter home-brewed beer at hand. He tried to affect a rugged charm, but succeeded only in appearing bewildered.

"They's a at it again, Bean." Yager scratched his chin, scowling at the feel of uneven stubble. It had seemed to Yager as a young boy that any man worth his salt could grow a strong, healthy beard so thick a bear could hide in it. As such, it was a great disappointment, one of many to come, when he came of age and short prickly hairs began to sprout up in random patches on his face, leaving some areas as smooth and pink as a babe's bottom. Overall, it left him looking rather wild and hysterical what with the lined years upon his cheeks and forehead combining to give him a perpetual quizzical frown. It was one of the many reasons people tended to avoid Yager and if he came close to a woman, hat held meekly in his stubby fingers, she was more likely to throw coins in the floppy old Stetson than talk to him.

Bean flicked a ragged ear toward Yager's scratchy voice and then went back to grazing through the waist high grasses.

He had long since grown accustomed to Yager complaining and tended to ignore him more often than not.

"I'm not a *educated* man, Bean, but I knows they is up to something." Yager stressed the word "educated," proud of his vocabulary. In fact, he would often go on for hours talking about how he felt the entire system of learning was a gov'ment, as he called it, plot against the working man. Yager always failed to point out even to himself that he was not and never had been a working man. The spare change he made in a day from trying his best to sweet talk any beauty, which would not have appealed to even the most desperate of women, earned him often times enough for his daily bread.

Bean sidled further away the longer Yager talked.

There was a quick burst of rustling a hundred yards north and Yager leaned forward with his boney elbows on his equally pointy knees, eyes eagerly intent on the swaying grasses. He muttered something incoherent, shot Bean a sideways glare, and took a slobbering gulp of his brew. By now in life his taste buds had long since been seared away by the vile liquid. When he had, years back, taken his first experimental sip he had woken days later with a raw and burning throat and swore he had seen God.

"Dang varmints." Yager tossed the mug aside and stood up, his knees creaking as loudly as the wobbly porch boards beneath his feet. "Stupid dogs, pah!"

A sound strangely reminiscent of sawing filtered up to Yager's ears. He scowled even deeper and thought back, his lips sucking into his mouth like a toothless hag. A year ago, Yager had started noticing disappearances, mostly little inconsequential items. At first he had thought nothing of it as often several days later what ever was missing showed up again. It wasn't until the disappearances became more frequent that Yager began to pay them any heed. He suspected something a bit peculiar might be going on after his hammer had gone missing and days later he had woke to the sound of it pounding fiercely beneath his floorboards. As more noises erupted over time from under the ground, he began to suspect the prairie dogs. Though what they were doing, he hadn't any clue.

It was as nightfall was closing in that Yager finally gave up his vigil and went inside his one room shanty. He turned a full circle and surveyed his domain proudly, his narrow chest puffing up with a craftsman's pride. He stopped short on the second turn to gape impotently at Bean who had long since come inside and laid down upon Yager's straw bedding. What followed had long become a nightly routine for them both.

"Get off, get off. How many times do I have to tell you, Bean?" Yager waved his skinny arms wildly through the air.

Bean rolled an eye toward him, snorted, and promptly feigned sleep.

"Yager B. Hines is *not* a man to be trifled with!"

Bean snored.

"That's it!" Yager pushed and pulled, grunted and cursed. He rammed his shoulder repeatedly into the donkey's backside. He tried to lever him off the bed with a board and even resorted to a bout of pleading on bended knee that quickly escalated to impossible threats. Bean never budged.

Panting, Yager finally conceded temporary defeat and stomped onto the porch again, this time in a fine rage. He was just beginning to roll a bit of tobacco when the sound of boards clattering and a high-pitched whine rang through the night. It was soon accompanied by the deep baritone snores that can only come from an overweight and contented donkey.

Yager sucked in his lips, his left eye twitched.

The world seemed to like to pick on him, Yager figured as he stood on the porch and smacked his gums with indignation. Well then, he thought in a manner he decided was quite heroic, he was just going to pick right back! Hitching up his pants, Yager spun back in the house, grabbed his beaten Stetson, and plopped it on his head. He struck a pose, aiming for dignity, but falling short when his hat slipped past his eyes to rest on his nose. From behind him, Bean snorted.

"I'm putting a stop to this illegal thievin'. There's going to be respect for me in these parts!" Yager grabbed a stout walking stick, having long ago run out of ammunition for his rifle. He glowered at the rustling grasses and hopped down from his porch, cursing his repeated failure to build stairs when a sharp pain shot up from his ankle.

Yager slung the stick against his shoulder and marched stiff-legged into the prairie. He felt like a ten-foot tall cowboy, ready to take on the world and fight to the death. Yager B. Hines, lean and mean, with the world trembling beneath his boots. He sneered confidently around the plains with each swaggering step up until he abruptly fell through a loose covering of soil and landed on a pile of timber shavings. A clod of dirt tumbled shortly after him and plopped on his head. As he was shaking the dirt from his eyes, Yager caught glimpse of a long face peering down at him.

"Bean! Why, I should've known it was you. You cheat, you liar, you fiend! You *pushed* me!" Yager waggled his knobby fist in the air and his scratchy voice squeaked painfully high.

Bean, for his part, plastered his ears flat to his scalp and brayed, showing wide yellow teeth. He shook his head, ears and lips flapping loudly. *Liar,* he seemed to say.

"Get me out of here, Bean." Yager stood up, his footing precarious on the rotting debris. He was trying his best to regain what dignity might be left to him, but his oversized hat slipped again. He was forced to settle it upon his ears, pushing them away from the side of his head and making him look all the more bemused.

The donkey gave one last shake and bray before he placed his footing carefully along the sinkhole. He made his slow way down, but instead of toting Yager back up again he kept walking past, all the while making a sound that was suspiciously similar to laughter. He passed out of sight beneath a dark overhang of dirt and grass.

It was as Yager sputtered at Bean's dwindling behind that he realized he had unwittingly fallen into the entry of an impressively large tunnel. It was just barely wide and tall enough for Bean to be able to walk comfortably through, but Yager had to twist at the waist and crabwalk in order to fit, shuffling awkwardly from side to side on bent knees.

The thought came into Yager's mind that he was directly in line with the most deadly portion of Bean, who had been aptly named early in life. With fear hastening his movements and oiling his joints, Yager managed to crawl over and around Bean to take the lead. He breathed a great sigh of relief not a minute too soon.

"Ungentleman-like, Bean," Yager drawled as he fumbled blindly ahead. The light from the tunnel entrance had quickly fled the further along they went. He lamented the loss of his walking stick, having dropped it when he plummeted into what essentially accounted for a prairie dog foyer.

Yager's mind was often akin to molasses with thoughts slow in forming so it was a long time before he wondered at the size of the tunnel. "These are some mighty big varmints," he muttered eventually and was reassured to hear Bean snort behind him. The thought of turning back began to nag persistently at him. Just as he was becoming accustomed to the darkness and about to return to the relative safety of his shack, a soft yellow of wavering light began to tinge the earthy edges of the tunnel. They were slowly, on account of Yager's contorted walk, approaching a bank of lit candles that were surrounded by several small figures.

There was a loud squeak from the shadows and four prairie dogs, of normal shape and size, ran hysterically around the tunnel, bumping into one another and the walls until they collapsed in an exhausted heap at Yager's feet.

"What in tarnation!" Yager yelled and shuffled away as much as he could. He backed into the candles, tripped and grabbed wildly at the air as he fell. His fingers snatched a heavy woolen blanket that had gone missing weeks before and it followed him to the ground, revealing at last what the prairie dogs had been building.

Yager came face to face with a crudely sculpted mud statue of himself. His dirty double was on his knees, arms stretched high and fisted. It was a pose that seemed vaguely familiar to him, but he couldn't place it at the moment.

The prairie dogs inched closer to Yager, poked him carefully with their nimble paws then huddled several feet away to chitter amongst themselves. After a consensus seemed to be reached, they swarmed the Yager's muddy doppelganger with handfuls of moss, which was carefully placed in the same patchy pattern as his own scraggly beard.

"What the dang tootin' is going on here!" Yager yelled. The prairie dogs squeaked and ran for cover again. He glowered at the lot of them, his chin jutted out with indignation, but a light slowly began to flicker in his eyes. Could it be? Could Yager B. Hines be immortalized in mud, a god to lowly varmints, but a god nonetheless? And what did gods get? Respect, admiration, and not least of all, worship.

"Yahoo!" Yager leapt into the air, dragging the blanket with him. His spindly legs flailed and he danced on his toes. His head bumped the roof of the tunnel time and again, flinging dirt in every direction. "Finally, the world knows that I am a man worthy of respect, ace-high! I am…I am…"

It was like listening to an organ come to a stuttering halt as Yager's eyes took in the rest of the newly revealed scene. The woolen blanket Yager had danced with mere seconds before had hidden a lovingly sculpted image of Bean, his long face set in a regal expression. The familiarity of the dirty double's posture was recognized at long last as the begging stance he took each night to try out of sheer desperation to evacuate Bean from his bed. The prairie dogs had misinterpreted it as worship. Bean was their god.

As Yager sputtered and fumed, the prairie dogs ventured back out from their various hiding places and circled reverently around Bean. The donkey flicked his tail and eyed them curiously while gnawing on an exposed root in the tunnel wall. It didn't take much prodding for him to be led to a raised pedestal overfilled with cut grasses.

"Darn you, Bean. Get down from there! Right now!" Yager was beginning to turn an alarming shade of beet red that quickly took on epic proportions of color when all but one of the prairie dogs knelt in front of Bean with excited and reverential squeaks. The standing dog darted over to a haphazard pile of junk and dug energetically for several minutes while Yager continued to rave in ever-increasing higher pitched tones. It was as Yager's limbs were especially akimbo and he was reaching critical meltdown that the prairie dog scampered over to his feet, a dangling scrap of cloth in his mouth.

"What do you want, you ungrateful pest? You filthy thieving varmint four-flushers! What is that in your mouth?"

The item in question was dropped quickly to the ground and the prairie dog dashed back to the relative safety of the worshipping mound of rodents beneath Bean.

Yager glowered at what appeared to be a crudely stitched collar.

"What the…" Yager picked it up, waved it about a few times experimentally, and glowered between it and the prairie dogs. He pried open his memory and peered blearily back to his

99

childhood when his mother had dragged him a time or two to church. Did they really want him to…? Moments passed with the dogs watching him expectantly.

He deliberated while glaring fiercely at Bean who in turn munched contentedly on the pile of grasses from atop his pedestal, face innocent. Yager felt he had a conundrum, though he had no working definition or knowledge of the word. He came out West to be respected and feared, to make a mark on the world, but found himself stranded, thanks to Bean he added silently, in the middle of nowhere. Now that smug beast of burden was getting worshipped by a group of prairie dogs that wanted him, Yager B. Hines, to be their priest. More long moments of deliberation followed and he experimentally tried it on, just to see if it fit, he told himself.

Yager tapped his chin, scratched his stubble and put on his most intimidating scowl. He examined his last memory of church again. The priest had gotten a lot of attention from the congregation that day. To Yager, attention meant respect. He cleared his throat noisily. Maybe just a word or two to try it out, he told himself.

"We are gathered here today…" His squeaky voice was magnified loud and deep by the cavernous tunnel and it boomed through the air. The prairie dogs quivered, clearly impressed and awed. A smug smile at their reactions tugged at the corners of Yager's mouth and he threw his arms dramatically into the air. and continued the world's first prairie dog sermon. Bean slept through it all.

The Cowgirl and the Cooters
Paul Wittine

A young cowgirl drew her six shooters,
And pointed them at two old cooters.
I'll blow you away,
On the very day,
You once again call my breasts hooters!

THE FIRST TEXAS TWISTER
Magnolia Belle

This tale begins before we knew anything about the space-time continuum and how easily it could be ripped. This tale begins shortly before the Civil War, in the high plains of Texas, before there even was a city named Amarillo. Buffalo and Native Americans had worked out a respectable balance between themselves, allowing each to live and prosper. Buffalo fed the humans, and humans thinned out the weakest from the herds.

Then, in the midst of this utopia, Europeans pushed their way past the Appalachian Mountains, past the Mississippi River, and headed toward the west coast. Some of them stopped along the way, settling in the midst of the buffalo and Native Americans, building homes and starting farms.

We all know this is where the trouble began for the Great West. But, what most of us don't know is that this is also the birth of the killer tornado.

Let me take you back...

The Kiowa, White Fox, sat outside his wife's lodge, his nervous eyes searching the wide-opened blue sky. As shaman of his village, the Kiowa elder had a certain reputation to uphold. He interpreted spirit dreams, knew which plants and herbs made good medicine, and conducted marital counseling on a surprisingly regular basis.

But that morning, his brow furrowed in worry. Murmuring throughout the camp grew louder each day about the lack of rain. The prairie grass crackled and broke when anyone walked on it. The buffalo moved further north to find water, making hunting difficult. They would have to move the village if this kept up. But, before they resigned themselves to yet another move, they waited on him to DO something.

The old man had tried everything in his power to affect the weather, but nothing had worked — not the sweat lodge, not the sacred smoke, not the dream quest for a vision. The simmering heat brought sweat to his wrinkled face, which trickled down his leathery cheek. Lost in thought, he didn't feel it. He considered the sky, spread unadorned without even the wispiest of clouds;

no soft breeze stirred the feathers in his graying braids. He grunted once, as if coming to a decision.

"Little Crow, come here," he addressed a young brave strolling by.

"Yes, father?"

"Tell the village to prepare themselves. This afternoon, I shall perform our sacred rain dance. The people must fast until then. And send the dancers to me."

"Very well." Little Crow nodded and went to his task.

White Fox bowed his head, hoping desperately this would work. If it didn't, they would be forced to move tomorrow or the next day.

Ruthie Simpson pulled hard on the reins, bringing their four mules to a stop. The covered wagon shuddered for a moment, sending puffs of dust pluming to the sky. Five other wagons stopped behind her.

"What now?" Her husband, William, walked up and rested one hand on the wheel.

"We oughta settle here," Ruthie explained.

"Here?" He made a slow turn, studying the horizon. Heat waves shimmered several yards ahead, across dry grass and brown shrubs. A quarter mile away, a small hill rose, the only landmark in the otherwise flat, barren landscape. *"Here?"* he repeated.

"Yep. Here." The flint-jawed woman nodded once, put the reins down and tucked a rebellious wisp of brown hair underneath her bonnet.

"Why'd we stop?" Red Parker came up behind William. "Mule go lame?"

"Naw." William pulled a bandana from his back pocket, lifted his stained hat with one hand and wiped his brow with the other. "Ruthie wants to settle here."

"You're joshing. Right?" By now, the other men had joined the discussion, all looking up at Ruthie, perched on the wagon seat, her lips in a thin line.

"Just 'cuz I'm a curious ol' cuss," Red smiled to disguise his anger at the most stubborn woman he'd ever met, "why here, Mz. Simpson?"

"Just a feeling I have in my bones."

"A feeling in your bones," he echoed, trying to keep his opinion of her suspect sanity out of his voice.

"There's no water here, wife," William explained.

"There was and there will be," she disagreed.

"How do you know that?"

"See that creek bed? That means there's water." She pointed a little distance away.

Sighing, William walked to it, pulled out his Bowie knife, and plunged it into the gully. After digging for a few moments, he stood and called back. "If there was water, it ain't been here in a long, long time. It's nothing but dry dirt for several feet down."

"Sorry, Mz. Simpson, but this place won't do." Red shook his head.

"It will, too!" Ruthie jumped down from the wagon, landing on her feet with a heavy thud. She stood with her arms akimbo, in her favorite arguing stance. "I know what I know, and this is the place!"

"She'd out-argue God," Red muttered under his voice.

"There was water here, and there'll be water here again. It's gonna rain. Just see if it don't!" Ruthie ignored her husband's pained expression at being embarrassed yet again in front of their friends.

"I'd like to knock you into next Tuesday," he threatened under his breath. But, there were too many witnesses, she had a powerful left hook, and she stood a little taller and a little wider than he did. "We're wasting daylight," he said out loud.

"I'm telling you! It's gonna rain!" In her proclamation, she raised her hands skyward and shook both fists. "IT'S GONNA RAIN!"

She spoke with such fevered conviction that the weakest minded of the wagon train wondered if she might not be right —somehow.

On the other side of the low hill a quarter mile away, unbeknownst to the wagon train, White Fox assembled the musicians and dancers. They smoked the pipe and washed in the sacred smoke. After that, he led them to the center of the ring

formed by the people.

The drums began first, throbbing in slow rhythm. Flutes, piercing and sweet, joined in. Some people had eagle bone whistles and blew them.

White Fox danced, one moccasin stomping into the dirt, and then the next, raising small red puffs of dust. His braids jostled at each step. The younger dancers spun around in circles to the music, and all the people watched the sky. After half an hour of dancing, White Fox scanned the horizon. Nothing. After an hour, still nothing. Feeling the pain and weariness in his joints, the old man felt he couldn't continue. Perhaps they would have to move after all. In one last burst of strength, he held his arms up, his fists clenched, and let out a cry, begging for rain to fall.

As it happened, Ruthie raised her fists at the exact same moment. A man agreeing with a woman, and a Native American agreeing with a settler, all less than a mile apart, proved too much for the universe to handle. That is when the space-time continuum ripped and a new thing came to earth. If people had listened carefully and had understood, they would have heard a slow wind in the distance. The prairie grass dipped slightly. Even without clouds, the sky grew a bit darker blue.

The Kiowa and the settlers felt a change in the atmosphere. Looking to the west, the sky began to transform; the wind picked up. The dark blue turned an eerie green. The eerie green turned to pitch black. Thunder growled, low and dangerous. The Kiowa had seen storms before, but nothing like this — ever. Lightning clawed the ether with golden talons. Hail as big as a child's fist fell, sending the people scrambling for their lodges. And the *wind* — the wind turned from a gentle breeze to a monster. White Fox felt certain the Wind Spirit was paying a personal visit.

The howling gale deafened ears. The hail pelted down mercilessly. And then nothing — nothing except skin-crawling silence. Even the grass stood still.

"What in tarnation?" William wondered out loud as he peeked out the back of his wagon.

"Told you it was gonna rain!" Ruthie crowed in her triumph and climbed out. She ran several yards towards the clouds, eager to be the first one to meet the rain.

"Get back in here!"

Ignoring William, she saw it — the biggest, blackest, vilest cloud covering the western horizon. It dropped lower and lower, until it formed a belly. The belly twisted and writhed, pointing closer to the ground with each second, sending debris piercing the air. Before Ruthie had time to run to shelter, the twister jumped the small hill, jumped the dry creek bed, and landed on top of her.

When it disappeared, no sign of Ruthie could be found. William wasn't quite sure how he felt about that (until he found her on the trail four days later — on a Tuesday). With all the ensuing rain, the Kiowa didn't have to move; the grass greened up and the buffalo returned. White Fox gained even more status with his people and died several years later as a revered elder.

And now you know how killer tornados were born — combined stubborn agreement from polar opposites — in *spite* of the obvious (which some people call faith and some stupidity). *And*, you have proof that someone really can be knocked into next Tuesday.

He Came From Wild West Country
Linda Lee Booth

He came from wild west country
As the sun sets over the hills
In a cabin down in a green valley
To avoid his Income Tax bills

Living it up at night time
Giving the barn dances a bash
Made him very quickly out of pocket
Made him very quickly out of cash

But this to him was not a problem
He continued having his do
Until one day they caught him
The Inland Revenue

106

Skunked

Lyn McConchie

"Do I haf'ta?"

I glared at my ten-year-old son. "Yes, you do. I don't care that we live far from eastern civilization. It's 1865 not 1765. The schoolmaster arrives next week and as soon as he's settled in, you'll attend classes three days a week."

Robert glared rebelliously but I was adamant. "You'll not only attend class," I told him. "You'll work and learn. If the teacher reports that you're lazy, rude or inattentive, your father will have something to say to you. Do you understand me?"

My son isn't a fool, he knew that his father wouldn't bother to reason, he'd just reach for his belt. So, unless Robert could think of some really convincing reason why he was unable to attend the school, he'd go — and he'd be polite to the new teacher and work hard.

After all, it was a miracle we'd found a teacher, the area is lawless still — and the Comanche are always with us — with this part of Texas still sparsely settled. But we'd built a schoolhouse, with a two roomed school building beside it, three outdoor privies. There was a rainwater tank — that leaked constantly — providing a deep semi-liquid mud puddle beside it that was often abused by mischievous pupils. And we'd fenced everything in with a solid, high fence that sloped slightly outwards to stop any problems with roaming bulls. And at need, teacher and pupils could fort up and fight off an attack, until their kin could ride to the rescue.

I smiled as Robert trudged off. I'd had an excellent education and I wanted no less for my son. I'd been one of those to interview the new teacher and he had impressed me. I suspected that his enthusiasm would be imparted to his pupils as well.

"Robert? It's early, are you leaving now?"

"Yes, Mr. Patterson's telling us all about the Romans."

I hid a smile. I'd been right. Mr. Patterson did impart his own enthusiasm to his pupils and what was more they liked the man. It was infuriating therefore that a year later he had to take several months leave. His father in Fort Worth was gravely ill and there was no one else to care for him. But our neighbor had a solution of sorts.

"There's man we could hire. He's an educated man, not a trained teacher, but he'd keep them from forgetting everything they've learned."

We hired Jonathon Weber on a month by month basis and found it a bad bargain. The girls were afraid of his sarcastic tongue and the boys hated him. Robert was increasingly reluctant to attend school but I insisted. Until the day when he returned home in only the time it would have taken him to ride there and back.

"Why are you home so early?"

"Skunk got into the school."

"A skunk?" We had them in the area and it was true they often hid under buildings, but that was the idea of the fence. The gate could be barred from the inside and locked from the outside, and it was custom to keep it secure at all times.

"How could a skunk get into the property?"

"Dunno, maybe Mr. Weber left the gate open."

It was possible. Meanwhile it would be several days before the schoolrooms were habitable again. Actually it was longer than that. The smell faded to where Mr. Weber would teach within the building, and—a day later—another skunk made its presence felt.

This time Mr. Weber was certain that he hadn't permitted the animal to sneak in. He yelled at the girls, believing, I think, that they could be more easily frightened into talking if they knew anything. Apparently none of them did, or if they did, they weren't as scared of him as he'd hoped. He turned to threatening the boys, saying that he'd beat them all if no one confessed.

Robert's friend, Martin Hindsaw, promptly remembered an earlier lesson and quoted the Magna Carta, the section about denying no man justice. Mr. Weber knocked him down, Martin stood up, left, and mounting his horse, rode for home where he reported events. His father, Colonel Hindsaw, is English, and, so far as he could see, his son had been unjustly threatened, then assaulted for quoting a document the Colonel held in great respect. He went to the school and said that if Mr. Weber wanted to retain his job he was on notice to do nothing to any pupil if he had no proof of wrongdoing.

The following day a skunk was again found under the school buildings.

Mr. Weber was angry and careless and this time it wasn't only the school that received a baptism when it was chased out. That did it. The temporary teacher wasn't going to be beaten by a group of children. He had a score to settle and if he could catch them bringing in a skunk he could settle it on his terms.

He took to locking the school gate at all times, counting the children in and out, checking saddlebags and any bundle of clothing in case it held a black and white intruder. He was sure that the fence was too high and at the wrong angle to be climbed, but however the skunks were still appearing, every time the school became useable again another skunk appeared to render it uninhabitable.

After three months Mr. Patterson was due back to teach from the following Monday and Mr. Weber had taught a bare handful of days over the period. But over the same time I'd been listening, both to Mr. Weber and to the children. As I say, I've had a good education, and that included tales of the Romans and their battles, also a popular topic for Mr. Patterson. Besides which, it's bad for children to believe their parents fools – even if the teacher is.

On the Friday I gathered the Colonel, my husband, and several other parents and we rode to the school shortly before the children would finish their class for the day.

"Mr. Weber. I felt that it would be a good idea to discover how it is that the school is so infested with skunks."

There was a distinct sneer in his reply. "Of course, madam, if you believe you can."

I walked to the bookcase, reached down a book and opened it, showing the large hand-tinted plate to the Colonel.

"A ballista, by Jove. Do you think...?"

A neighbor peered at the picture, "What's a ballista?"

"A sort of catapult," the Colonel told him. "The Roman's used them, you can toss huge rocks a long way with one of those."

He turned to look at me. "Where would it be?"

I smiled, led everyone out of the school enclosure and up to a small copse of scrub oak nearby, I thrust bodily into that and, holding a bush aside showed them a small version of the ballista hidden under cut branches. Mr. Weber turned puce.

"Nonsense. Certainly you could throw things over the school wall using such an engine. But a skunk would be badly injured when it landed and none of the filthy little brutes ever showed such damage."

I saw light dawn on the Colonel and held my tongue. Let him be the person to explain it.

"Of course not, man. Because as you said," here he laughed heartily.

"They were filthy little brutes. Whoever used this machine made certain to drop the skunk in that large mud puddle by the schoolroom door. I'd expect the beast to have been fed a small amount of alcohol beforehand so that, as long as it was neither hurt nor frightened, it wouldn't react. But speak the truth, wasn't each skunk that you saw, very muddy?"

The teacher nodded then ground his teeth. "I still don't believe it."

The Colonel snorted and spoke that immortal line that none of us present that day have ever forgotten. He pointed decisively to the ballista.

"You're wrong, Weber, this was exactly how the pest was flung!"

Good Business
Aurelio Rico Lopez III

When aliens take over the wild, wild West, no one except the mortician smiles.

pine coffins line street
outnumbered and outgunned
Martians invade town

The Film Cowboy
Paul Wittine

The greatest cowboy
In Living Technicolor
John "Marion" Wayne

110

SHOWDOWN AT SAN MARGUERITE
H. Earl Wilkinson

Even a sightless, scentless, senseless human could have figured out that matters would have to be settled by a showdown in San Marguerite. On the master's last trip to town, I figured it out in five minutes.

Men glared at each other as they lit cigars at the bar, women wearing long skirts whispered as they traveled the Main Street shops, and boys ran out of the city school, whooping all the way....

But the smells of frying chicken, roasting jalapenos, and baking tortillas said it all for me — it was time for a Tex-Mex showdown in the No Way Corral.

Apparently some narrow-eyed people who'd come to build the railroads had brought the tradition with them — that of cookery combat. I didn't care if the tradition came from the Dog Star above. Showdowns were what every dog dreamed off — lots of fresh meat, lots of distracted humans, and a guaranteed full belly.

The humans held these showdowns to keep up appearances with the town over the border - a mutually agreed upon way to avoid this 'war' thing going on right now.

It didn't hurt either that the winners made a killing at their local restaurants.

"So there's a prize for the chickens who survive the longest?" the rooster asked for the thirteenth time from the cage in the back of the wagon. Apparently, freshly killed meat was best for the showdowns. "Us versus the Mexican chickens?"

I growled, half-tempted to take matters into my own teeth despite the master and mistress on the seat beside me. "Yes."

I could've told them that they and their Mexican counterparts were going to the butcher's block in town later today, but why? They would only make a huge ruckus in the back, shed more feathers, and smell even worse than usual. Why should I encourage them to exercise off any of that delicious fat? Nothing was more delectable than chicken — except for a good side of beef.

Besides, listening to their excuses for plotting – when

they could remember them one minute to the next – helped pass the hour long ride into town more quickly...

A low, throaty voice — the rooster, most likely - started. "We're going to need cows. Lots of cows."

"But it's never been done so it can't be done. You can't do something that's never been done unless it's been done..." The next chicken clucked so fast that I bet its head was spinning.

"What's a cow?" The last chicken was just stupid.

"Has someone cut your head off? Stop running around and listen! Cows are really big. If they run over the other chickens, we'll win the prize!"

"Oh, you mean the giant grass chewers?" The fast-talking chicken asked.

"Yes."

"Grass chewers run?" the stupid one sounded amazed. "I thought they were black and white rocks."

"It's simple. We'll make them an offer they can't refuse – here's the plan."

Between the warmth of the late morning sun and the rhythmic bouncing of the wagon seat, the chickens' clucking eased away into relaxing oblivion.

I didn't care as I dozed off. Since when were chickens significant, anyway?

Sooty air — mixed with the smells of something I'd really like to roll in — suddenly drifted into my dreams. I half-opened an eye and saw that the edge of town was already in sight.

"It's them — the Stinking Badge Bandits! We're gonna die!" the mistress wailed, flailing about her with her favorite cast-iron skillet. She had a curious habit of taking it with her everywhere she went, insisting that it was an educational tool.

The master ducked with a skill born of long practice and cast a look behind him at the plume of greasy black smoke snaking up to the sky. "Ah, 'tis nothing but a tiny flicker of smoke, mother. And you have a cooking contest to win, don't you?"

112

"A tiny flicker, eh? Tiny flicker? And just what do you think a farmstead being put to the torch looks like?!" the mistress cried. "This will all end in tears — I just know it!"

It had been maybe five minutes since she'd last made that pronouncement — she was having a good day.

A huge gathering of humans in their Sunday finest – calico dresses and bonnets, polished boots and buckles – gathered so tightly around the western side of the corral that I couldn't see the fence. The eastern side was blocked out by another group in bright red and orange of shawls and blanket-capes, topped with sombreros of woven blues and greens.

The master and mistress cut behind the corral and the stands raised for the occasion to the animal picket lines behind them. I never understood why humans generally avoided the rich, earthy, luscious smells of steers and cows...?

"Por favor, senor, but can you spare a little corn?" a mouse squeaked at me as the master argued with the local sheriff over picketing fees and the chickens squawked furiously at the nearby cows. "We're wasting away here in Margueriteaville!"

I growled at the mouse, annoyed by its painfully high-pitched voice. It was too small to eat, and, even worse, the wretch thought I was stupid. "That town's to the north — this is San Marguerite. Nice try. The chickens deserve a last meal."

The mouse shrugged and joined its fellows along with the spiders and horseflies lining the nearby corral fence to watch the show.

It didn't take long for the humans to begin the festivities.

The local mayor stood up on a barrel inside of the corral. "Welcome to the third battle of San Marguerite — a showdown between chickens here at high noon!" His declaration was met with furious applause on both sides once the translator had finished.

"But first — let's meet our panel of culinary experts. We've gathered the good, the bad, and the ugly to pronounce judgment on our eager competitors."

On the raised platform behind the corral, a wavering drunkard, a very curvaceous woman, and a grizzled, ancient cowboy sat at a table laid with human utensils.

The woman — very buxom and wearing a tight, low-cut red dress — stood up at her table and waved to the crowd. The golden heart-shaped pendant gleamed brightly. She took a deep breath and called out, "Hiya boys!"

Every man in the audience waved right back. Curiously, the master didn't seem to feel the mistress' frying pan this time. She ignored him and stormed forward, slipping under the fence just as her Mexican counterpart did the same.

Both women cast evil glares at their mates back in the crowd.

For my part, I wove my way through the crowd until I was behind the corral. I wanted a closer look at the meat-to-be. The town butcher waited next to the mayor with cleaver and block at hand. As I watched, he turned and lifted the master's cage of chickens.

"Too bad you won't get a chance to compete!" the rooster crowed, bobbing his head up and down. "Guess dogs just aren't up to the challenge. Guess what they say is true."

All around him in the cage, the chickens ran and ran in unorganized circles. I *hated* the very sight of it. Disordered, wild... they *needed* disciplining....

I growled, hunkering low to the ground. My legs tensed with the urge to spring. "And what do they say about dogs?"

"That they're really chicken!"

That was it. I rushed under the fence and sprang at that cocky cock, barking the special bark passed down through generation of herding dogs.

The rooster, I was disappointed to see, was unimpressed even as I bounced against the sharp metal mesh and his world started wildly gyrating.

But the butcher was. He yelled and let go of the cage, flinching away from me. The rooster and his counterparts flew through the air. When they came down, their cage hit the hard stones lining the fire-pit at an angle.

Four chickens and a rooster hurried out through the now-open door.

"Get the chickens!" The cry went up throughout the crowd – some concepts knew no language barrier – and a dozen volunteers slipped under the fence to give chase.

I ran. I barked. So much disorder — could — not — be — endured!

Somehow, during the running, tripping, and yelling, the

other chicken cage was opened too. A second rooster entered the fray and I turned my barking circles in on the two birds facing off on the worktable covered in cooking ingredients.

The Mexican rooster crowed evilly as he circled around the master's rooster. "Why are you smiling?" The foreign bird, though obviously bigger, seemed cautious before closing in for the fatal pecking.

"Because I know something you don't know." The rooster backed up into a glass jar which tipped over, coating him in golden cooking oil.

"And what is that?"

In a rush, the Mexican rooster lunged forward leading with a massive hooked beak.

"Where the dog is." The rooster jumped into a bowl and vanished from my sight.

I hated to prove the little devil right, but I had to get through the Mexican rooster to get to my troublemaker if I wanted to teach him a lesson.

As I grabbed foreign bird and threw him aside, the battlefield around me grew curiously...silent. The screaming and the obstacles had been increasing the last few minutes. Surely not all the chickens had been retrieved yet.

But, oh the smells... I inhaled deeply and shivered at the urge to roll over and over.

Twelve men on horseback had forced their way into the crowd while I had been preoccupied. Although filthy, each man held a raised rifle to his shoulder and had multiple six-shooters at his belt. Tarnished badges dripping black filth were pinned to each of their chests.

The biggest rider dismounted and grabbed the mistress where she stood nearby, her face red with rage. Curiously, the master had never left his original place at the edge of the corral. His eyes were wide with horror at this development, but a strange little smile suddenly twitched at his lips.

A different sort of rage blasted through my heart. The mistress? My mistress — she must be protected.

"We're the Stinking Badge Bandits. Bring out your valuables or this woman and a lot of other folk in this crowd'll be six feet under!" the leader shouted.

The mistress, even with a pistol raised to her temple, did

not take this news calmly. "See, Joseph, I *told* you it was the Stinking Badge Bandits! And phew do they ever...."

"They do not!" the master snapped back. "You always make stuff up!"

"Do to! You're not right here with a nose full of stink!"

"Excuse me, but we're trying to have a hold up here! Shut up, both of you, or the old woman gets it!"

I'd seen enough. I had to save the mistress... but if I rushed in there, the Bandit would just turn and shoot me with his gun. I'd seen guns. I knew what they could do.

Maybe I could get him to do me a favor.

Reaching up on the table with my forepaws, I grabbed the rooster by the scruff with my mouth and, before he could protest, I threw him with all my might at the Bandit's head.

His eyes went wide as the rooster — now glistening and sticky with oil and corn flour — flew closer and closer to him. For his part, the rooster squawked, crowed, and fouled himself, desperate to end this unnatural flight anyway he could.

Apparently, the head of the Stinking Badge Bandits did know when to hold them and when to fold them. Confronted by a hysterical yellow rooster, he yelled and threw up his hands. His wild shot at the bird — which had bounced off of the mistress' head — did miss the featherhead.

But, the shot was answered by thunderous hoof-falls from the north. I turned, unable to believe my eyes. Every single cow and steer from the picket lines had torn loose from their tethers and were stampeding directly at the corral!

The cows and their fellows charged through the area, and bandits, townspeople, and animals scattered and scrambled in every direction to avoid getting trampled. Punches were thrown, six-shooters spat, and other frying pans were brought into play to subdue the bandits. In the chaos, sparks from the two fire-pits flew into the air. Some landed on the corral fence and the nearby tables, setting them ablaze. It wasn't long before sparks from that fire reached the blacksmith shop nearby and set that ablaze too.

The mistress was doing just fine now, re-educating the head of the Stinking Badge Bandits at length about the virtues of bathing with her frying pan. I took my chance and ran over to the rooster.

116

It looked like the town had got its taste of the war it had been avoiding after all... and it had been saved by a yellow-bellied chicken?

That just didn't seem right.

"What did you tell the cows?" I yelped.

The rooster clucked happily at me. "That they'd win the big prize if they could beat us in a race when the gunshot sounded. And they beat us fair and square — and trampled the Mexican chickens in the process! Looks like we won the survival game after all!"

I gave him a second look, wondering just how stupid chickens really were.

That night, two donated cows were roasted to feed the exhausted crowd. The cows had won the 'big prize' of the butcher's block that I had promised to the chickens this morning. For his part, the master's rooster was disappointed to discover that I'd been telling stories and he hadn't won the prize after all.

I didn't care. Beef tasted much better than chicken, so this ending to my story suited me just fine.

ATTACKING THE IRON HORSE
Steve Doyle

The brave waited anxiously
Upon his fastest pony
For the menace of the prairie.

The white man's train
Roared across the plain
And drove the buffalo away.

When the Iron Horse came back
He would snare it by the stack
And drag it from the track.

The beast thundered through.
He charged in hot pursuit.
Round and round his lasso flew.

Yeah, he roped that stack.
He pulled up fast—
And flew from his pony's back.

He let go
After 'bout a mile or so.
Last time one of 'em tried that.

Missing Cowboys
Will Morton

See the buzzards out over the plain,
Bones and memories are all that remain,
And the old hitching post
Might as well be a ghost,
Those old cowboys I search for in vain.

The Farmer Takes a Wife
Timothy A. Sayell

"Pundetta, I'd like to see you for a moment, if I may," the schoolmarm sternly said.

"Yessum, Miss Strait."

"The rest of you are dismissed," the teacher announced. The children filed out of the schoolhouse as Pundetta reluctantly trudged up to the teacher's desk, her books hanging from her hand by means of a belt. "Uh, Pundetta, it's about this paper you turned in…"

"Yessum?"

"Well, you know, child, it was supposed to be a factual account of some ordeal a member of your family lived through…"

"Yessum."

"And it was not to be exaggerated or embellished," Miss Strait said firmly.

"Oh, no ma'am!" Pundetta cried. "It weren't exaggerated! Not one bit. Not a single member of my family has ever yet been found to fib. It's the family vanity, ma'am, and I shall proudly verify my veracity."

The schoolmarm regarded the student with a dubious and appraising gaze. "Very good then, if you'd be so kind. Explain to me the subject of your paper. Just speak freely."

"Yessum, I shall," the student said. "It all happened over Grand Gorge way, my Paw's got a cousin out thare name of Joe Diggs, but we all call him Uncle Joe. He's a good Joe, my Uncle Joe. But then somethin' terrible happened to him."

"And what was that?" Miss Strait asked.

"He fell for a high-falootin' filly! Her name was Priscilla Highbrow, but most folks call her Prissy. She's one of them rich and ritzy, hoity-toity Highbrows," Pundetta said sagely. "Mama says she's a no-good goosey who gabbles 'neath the gables with a gaggle of gossipin' girls, and I think I'd quite like to see that once. On account of I ain't too sure of how to gabble."

"Well, I wouldn't say that," the teacher commented dryly.

Pundetta looked up at the teacher with a perplexed frown, but it instantly left her and she continued. "Anyway, Uncle Joe done went and told Prissy how smitten he was with her. And you know what she done? She laughed at him! She laughed loud and long, chortled and chuckled, guffawed with great gusto, and snickered with snide insensitivity at my poor ol' Uncle Joe! Then she said he'd have to ascend his standing and stature among the state's society and that his only hope to such fine fortunes would be with a fruitful farm! Only then might she marry him."

"I see," said Miss Strait, nodding an understanding nod. "So, what did your Uncle Joe do about it?"

"Well, truth be told," said Pundetta, turning shamefully towards the floor. "He sought to sink his sorrow at the Silver Spur Saloon. And that...," here she raised one finger to stress the upcoming vital point. "...was where he run into a fella!"

"A fellow?"

Pundetta nodded. "A fella! The fella's name was Poole." She paused and frowned thoughtfully. "Don't rightly recollect what his first name was. I just remember that folks called him 'Dirty' Poole."

Miss Strait was dumbfounded. "Why did they call him 'Dirty' Poole?"

Pundetta shrugged. "He told Uncle Joe it was on account of his little dirt farm, which promised profitability if properly worked. Mr. Poole, apparently, couldn't work the place proper, on account of some shrapnel stuck in his spleen since the war, or so he said."

"I see," said Miss Strait, her understanding tone growing slightly strained.

"Well, Uncle Joe done bought the farm, and it was nearly the death of him. Turns out that fella Poole was a dirty one, all right! He done sold my Uncle Joe the single most inhospitable real estate in all of Grand Gorge!" She paused for a thoughtful moment. "Maybe in the whole west!"

"So, then what did he do?" Strait asked.

Pundetta considered it, one thoughtful finger tapping her chin. "Well, first off, he went to visit this old Injun medicine man, who lived in his teepee outside of town. I could never pernounce his Injun name rightly; I guess most white folk couldn't. As I recollect, it meant something like 'Him-Who-Has-Long-Face', but the townsfolk just called him Horace."

Miss Strait crossed her arms and asked, "What did he need the Indian for?"

"Well, ol' Injun Horace was old and wise, and Uncle Joe wanted his opinion on the situation," said Pundetta. "Well, ol' Horace's helpful hints all held that a heap of hard work and a hefty heart would harbor a healthy harvest! All he had to have was a horse to help with the plowin'. But Uncle Joe was in luck there, cause ol' Horace just happened to have one!"

"What a coincidence." Miss Strait remarked.

"Not really," Pundetta shrugged. "You see, handling horses was Horace's bag and he offered my Uncle a hard-working nag. But once the deal had gone through it was plain to see that this old gray mare weren't what she used to be..."

Miss Strait waggled one finger at the schoolgirl in warning. "Ah-ah, Pundetta! You're rhyming again!"

The girl grinned sheepishly behind one hand. "Oops, sorry, ma'am!"

The teacher looked at the student through narrow, suspicious eyes. "I've observed that you have a tendency to do that when you're on the cusp of stretching the truth."

Pundetta held up one hand solemnly while the other crossed her heart. "Taint no Texas tall-tale, ma'am, but total truth! I swear on the grave of my dear-departed Uncle Zeke Burroughs, who never got out of the Maple Hill Mine a-fore it collapsed."

"All right, all right!" said Miss Strait as she waved away her most recent suspicion. "So, your uncle bought a horse from this Indian?"

"Yessum!" Pundetta confirmed. "Ol' Fido was a tired old thing, but you could tell by just a-looking at her that she was a strong ol' horse in her day."

"Wait a minute." The schoolmarm held up one hand.

"Let me be sure I understand. The horse's name was Fido?"

"Yessum!" Pundetta nodded. "It seems the old Injun got a little confused with how white folk name their animals." She shrugged. "Anyway, poor ol' Fido wasn't much help with the plowin' or anything else, really. But Uncle Joe whiled away the weeks by working himself weary."

The teacher smiled and nodded encouragingly. "And did his efforts yield results?"

"Not even a weed," Pundetta sadly reported. She instantly brightened up and raised one finger with theatrical flair. "But that's when it happened!"

Miss Strait watched her expectantly, but the student remained still. "Well? That's when what happened?"

Pundetta grinned. "The Magnificent Professor Shameau and his Traveling Medicine Show passed by his farm on its way to Grand Gorge."

"Sham-o?"

"Yes! A clever, world-class chemist who wanders the west producing potions and elixirs to eliminate everyday ills!" Pundetta enthused. "The man is a justifiable genius, according to Uncle Joe."

Miss Strait looked shocked. "Don't tell me your uncle actually bought something from one of those traveling con artists!"

"Yessum, he did! And it weren't no con, neither." Pundetta insisted. "He bought a bottle of growth formula, made primarily from rose oil, guaranteed to grow gourds, produce potatoes, breed beans, cultivate corn, and virtually revive any vegetable you can envision!"

The teacher gaped at her skeptically. "And all this from rose oil?"

"That's what the man said."

"Well just what sort of rose was he using to make this stuff?"

"Who knows? Who knows? What sort of a rose do you suppose could give us an oil that makes other plants grow? I do not know and you do not know. But I know that its so, 'cause I was told it by my good Uncle Joe!"

"A-ha!" Miss Strait exclaimed, pointing an accusing finger. "More rhymes!"

Looking guilty, Pundetta slapped a hand over her mouth. Then she smiled, and said, "Sorry, ma'am. Got a might carried away." She cleared her throat conspicuously, then continued. "Anyway, he planned to try the growth formula first thing in the morning, and put it in the barn with his other farmin' tools. He was bankin' everything on that stuff. He'd spent just about all his savings on the farm, Fido, and the formula, just to try and impress ol' Prissy. I guess that's why Mama says love is many squandered things."

"Oh!" groaned Miss Strait.

The schoolgirl continued, nonplussed. "So Uncle Joe prayed for that formula to work and went to bed. He got up early the next morning and had a disastrous discovery! The formula fell into Fido's feed, and Fido fed on it!"

"You don't say? Well what, in the name of Tecumseh's peace pipe, did he do about that?" Miss Strait asked.

"Fortunately, the formula fixed up Fido into a factory fabricating the finest fertilizer from Philadelphia to Fort Wayne... and further!" Pundetta announced, her books swinging dangerously on their strap as she gestured enthusiastically. "The barn was simply packed with piles and piles of plant food, which he pitched into that problematic and unproductive patch."

Miss Strait nodded somberly. "Well, I suppose that brings an end to it then."

"You'd think so, ma'am, but no!" the student declared. "Three days later, he found the plant beds in full bloom, abounding with bounty! Three days after that, the gardens quit growing, having gained gargantuan size. The beans ballooned as big as bananas! The peapods puffed up to the proportion of pickles! Even the weeds were as long as whips! Which just goes to prove what my Paw always says."

"Why, what does your father say?"

"He says that when it comes to farmin', a turd on your land is worth two in the tush!"

"Pundetta!" Miss Strait exclaimed.

"Well he does!" Pundetta insisted defensively. "Anyway, word spread through town, and everyone came out to see the vegetables of his labors. He was recognized as the greatest green thumb in Grand Gorge. Folks offered him money for his harvest, then other folks offered him more, then other folks outbid them.

Mr. Clutchwell, the banker, offered to personally help Uncle Joe invest the money if he opened an account. Even them hoity-toity Highbrows took notice of him, perceiving him a prominent person-in-the-making. Even that Prissy passed the time of day with him. Everything seemed to be coming together for good ol' Uncle Joe. The world had beat a path to his door and was fast-becoming his oyster! There was only one thing left to, and he did it!"

Miss Strait frowned. "What did he have to do?"

Pundetta frowned back in astonishment. "Isn't it obvious? He had to weed it and reap!"

PERTY PUPS
Will Morton

The cowboys was laughin' at me,
Sayin', "Git right along, li'l dogies!"
But I said, "Hit the trail!"
An' my herd wagged their tails,
Each dogie a-barkin' with glee.

THE LUTENIST
Lindsey N. Williams

Archibald Crittington III's bum was aching. He had been sitting on a hard seat for what seemed like years. First it was the unpadded bunk on the ship from England, then it was a seat on the train from New York City to Pittsburgh, followed by a long and uncomfortable series of stagecoach seats from Pittsburgh to St. Louis, which was now only an hour away. His bottom felt like a pancake, and he did not relish the idea of spending the next few months on horseback, on his long journey to California. Perhaps if he had known the trip would be this uncomfortable, he would have stayed in London and taken his father's offer of a bank partnership.

Despite his outraged posterior, Archie had high hopes of enjoying America, the Land of Opportunity. His heart swelled at the thought of all the gold flowing through those new mining towns, and the percentage of it that might soon be his. The thought so inspired him that he found himself smiling. A plain girl, with a figure like a closed umbrella, on the seat opposite Archie's smiled back and blushed, thinking his grin was pointed at her. It wasn't, but it never hurt to be polite.

"Headed for St. Louis?" he said.

The blushing girl nodded and looked at her lap.

"Are you a schoolteacher?"

She shook her head and mumbled something.

"Sorry, I didn't catch that?" he said.

"I'm a nurse," she said.

"Ah. Noble profession. And I am a lutenist, a traveling minstrel on my way to fame and glory in the great untamed West. I have a cousin I'm to meet at the station, a singer and songwriter, and we're making the journey to California together to seek our fortune."

The girl blushed even harder.

Another of the coach's passengers, a coarse-looking man with ragged clothes and dirty hair, scowled at him.

"Some folks talk too much," the man said, and the cold anger in his voice ruined any pleasure Archie had gotten from the brief conversation. They all sat in uncomfortable silence for the rest of the trip.

It was early evening when the coach arrived at the station, and quite chilly. Archie helped the blushing young woman with her luggage, then returned for his own. He was most concerned with his lute, which the coach master had not allowed him to carry with him, but insisted that it be stowed with the rest of the bags and crates.

Archie had fretted over the lute's treatment. It was his most prized possession, and his passport to possible wealth and fame. When he had first heard the news of the great gold rush two years previous, he had seen the possibilities right away. In a rush, he had written to his cousin Charles in St. Louis, with his proposition. After all, how many skilled musicians were there likely to be on the American Frontier? And of those, how many classically trained lutenists?

The bench inside the coach station disappointed Archie's bottom yet again. It was hard and cold and flat. Charles had said he would send someone to meet Archie, so he settled his lute

onto his lap and waited. His tail bone felt like a mule-kicked dog.

The ugly brute from the coach came into the station and demanded directions to the outhouse. Once directed, he disappeared. Archie hoped to be met and gone before the man returned.

As it turned out, he was. Soon three men came in and looked around. The tallest of the three, a buckskin-dressed fellow with large moustaches, spoke up. "I'm here to meet someone from the five o'clock stage,"

As there were no other folks standing to greet the fellow, Archie stood, slung his lute over his shoulder, and held out a hand.

"Archibald Crittington," he said, "you may call me Archie."

The man took his hand and shook it. His grip was hard and strong. He looked at Archie, his eyes as hard as his grip, but twice as cold. "You're the, ah..." the man started.

"I'm the lutenist," Archie said.

"Shh," the man said, "I wouldn't go bragging about it right out loud like that, you want to get us shot?"

"Well," Archie said, bewildered. "I didn't know Americans were so particular, but very well. I'll just get my things."

The men led him to a group of horses tied up outside. They had one saddled and ready for him, too, and they all mounted and rode away.

Soon after they left, the ugly fellow from the coach came back and sat where Archie had just been sitting, and waited for the outlaws he was supposed to meet. When a dapper fellow with a gold pocket watch entered, looked around, and asked for Archie Crittington, the ugly fellow saw his opportunity. He decided this fat goose was a lot easier pickings than the local bank was bound to be, and to heck with the outlaws. So he stood, greeted the dapper fellow, followed him outside and rode double with him to the edge of town. There he shot him and stole his watch, his horse, and all his money, then headed north as fast as the horse would take him. He never missed an opportunity to do a little bit of lootin'.

Archie, knowing none of this, followed the other riders

to their camp. Already, he had begun to have the feeling that something had gone badly wrong and these men were not from his cousin Charles. The two folks waiting at the camp were just as cold-eyed and hard as the fellow with the moustaches and the two friends he'd brought to the station. One of them was a pug-ugly woman with a lazy eye.

"Hey, Henry, who's the dandy?" said the woman. "I thought you was goin' to meet a shooter from back East."

The man with the moustaches, Henry, said, "His name's Archie, and he says he's the lootin'est."

"I don't know if I believe all that," the woman said, looking Archie up and down. "Nobody that dresses that spiffy could possibly beat out ol' Creepy Jones when it come to lootin'."

"Well, I don't know about ol' Creepy bein' the lootin'est, but he's sure as heck the shootin'est. But I think we'll give Archie the chance to prove hisself tomorrow at noon, at the bank downtown," Henry said. "You gotta give him credit for havin' guts, he said he was the lootin'est right out loud in the stagecoach station, big as life and twice as loud."

Archie swallowed hard; his stomach was trying to crawl back up his throat to make a run for it. He was now beginning to see where things had gone wrong, but could not see how to make them right again. He knew it would be a bad idea to disillusion these roughs, as they seemed the type to kill a fellow for knowing too much. On the other hand, he had no intention of robbing any banks. He had come to America to make his fortune, not to steal it. He was a musician, and peaceful by nature, and had never before needed an escape plan. He needed one now.

But necessity is the mother of invention, so Archie made polite conversation around the fire and resolved to make his escape plan once everyone had gone to sleep for the evening.

He took out his lute and strummed quietly for a couple of minutes. When nobody complained, he continued, strumming and picking a little louder.

"Say, do you know any real songs?" asked the woman, whose name was Pretty Mary.

"Of course, I know a great many," Archie said.

"Well, then. Play us one. If we like it, we won't shoot you," Pretty Mary said.

This was quite an incentive. Archie played one about

Robin Hood, hoping the lyrics about jolly highway robbery might go down well.

It did. There was a general agreement among the outlaws, and they asked for a couple more. Archie obliged them.

Soon the sun fell behind the horizon, sinking like a stone in a bucket of milk. Archie played until his fingers were sore, and when the outlaws tired of music, he put away his lute.

"It's suppertime," Henry said. He took out a poke and opened its drawstring. "Here, Archie. Have some beef jerky." He held out what looked like a mummy's tongue.

Archie, who hated beef jerky, said, "Certainly, I love beef jerky." He took it and stuck the foul salty thing into his mouth. He thought it might be best to keep his head down and his mouth shut and try not to attract any more attention. The woman, Pretty Mary kept a close eye on him, nonetheless. After a bit, Henry said enough was enough, so they turned in for the night.

One man was set to watch, and Archie lay on the hard cold ground, covered only with an oilskin. He lay there, thinking of schemes to distract the fellow long enough to jump on a horse and get away, and never noticed when he fell asleep.

He was awakened after a short time by someone crawling under his oilskin. Whoever it was smelled strongly of onions and whisky and sweat. Archie pretended to be asleep until he felt an arm wrap around his waist. Then he turned his head toward whoever it was.

"I beg your pardon, can I do something for you?" he whispered.

"Yeah, you sure can, pretty boy," a voice whispered back, and the face leaned in close, puckered for a kiss. Archie saw the lazy eye. It was Pretty Mary.

"No, no, I'm already engaged," Archie said, leaning away.

"What?" Pretty Mary said.

"Well, I'm very sorry, but I have a fiancee back in London." This was a lie, but Archie was too tired and overwhelmed to care.

"Well, I only thought, because you was the new guy an' all," Pretty Mary whispered. "I thought you might be lonely. And I seen you makin eyes at me all night." She squeezed his arm, feeling his muscles.

"Oh. Well, your, ah, matchless beauty must have, ah,

turned my head. Or something." From bad to worse. Archie felt his nose grow two inches.

"Oh, you," she simpered. Then her eyes grew alarmed. "Say, you wouldn't go and tell Henry about us, would you? Cause if you did, he'd be liable to kill us both. See, I'm Henry's old lady."

"Well," said Archie, thinking fast, "suppose I don't. Would you do something for me in return?"

"What?"

"Help me get out of here."

"Get out of here? What do you mean?"

"Well, you see, it's like this. I came to America to be a musician. I'm a lutenist, that instrument I play is called a lute. I'm not a bank robber at all. I've never even held a gun. And, being a musician, I have a strict coda conduct."

"Ohhh, I see," whispered Pretty Mary. "Well, don't that just beat all. Well, how about this, you don't tell Henry about you and me, and I'll help you get away if I can. But you gotta do something else for me, so I don't just go tell Henry you're a fake an' let him shoot you on the spot."

Archie had not counted on this turn. "And what might that be?" he whispered.

"Let me snuggle with you for a minute," Pretty Mary said. "It's so cold out here, and Henry always hogs the covers."

Archie thought about it. "Oh, very well," he said, and rolled back over.

With the morning's earliest light came a cold north wind, and Archie's oilskin was about as helpful as a shovel with a hole in it. The bandits' snoring was a terrible chorus to hear, but was enough to mask any sounds he might make escaping.

He took up his lute case and crept out of camp. After a dozen yards he began to breathe easier. It looked like he might make a clean getaway, after all.

"Where ya headed?"

Archie screamed and dropped his lute. Henry was crouched in the brush, picking his teeth with his left hand. His favorite gun, a double-barrel shotgun cut down until it looked like an overfed pistol, was in his right hand and pointed at Archie's belly. Archie didn't know much about shotguns, but he did know that when the hammers were back, one might be shot. The hammers on this one were back, so he assumed that he might be shot.

"Oh, ah, just to, you know. Take a morning stroll." His voice sounded right, but his lips were numb with fright. "There's nothing like the sound of morning bird-song to cheer a fellow."

"With yer git-tar?" Henry's voice dripped sarcasm.

"Well, yes. I mean, after all, you brought your gun with you."

"But you can't shoot rattlesnakes with a git-tar," Henry said.

Archie thought this might be a bad time to explain the differences between a lute and a guitar.

"Git back to camp and build up the fire," Henry fumed, his eyes smoldering.

"Right, great idea," Archie said. He wished, with every fiber of his being, that he were back in London, and vowed that if he got out of this ridiculous situation alive, that's exactly where he would go.

When they got back to camp, Pretty Mary was up, and had already stirred up the fire and set the coffee to boil. She stared hard at Archie.

"See?" Henry said, "Pretty Mary here don't trust you neither. You jus' keep your good eye on him, Pretty Mary."

She did. She watched Archie for most of the morning, her eyes following Archie much like iron filings follow a magnet. Her expression was about as hard and cold as a bunny rabbit.

Long about eleven o'clock, Henry said, "All right, y'all. Let's hunker down and plan this thing out." They all hunkered around what was left of the fire. "Okay, lookit." Henry took a stick from the little pile of kindling and drew a rough map in the dirt. "This here is the bank, and this is Main Street. Archie, can you read?"

"Of course," Archie said.

"Good. Can you write, too?"

"The two often, er, go hand in hand."

"So that's a yes? Good, cause I don't think any of the rest of us can. Anybody?"

There were head shakes all around.

"Okay, Archie, this part's your-un."

Urine? Archie thought, bewildered.

"You're gonna take this-here scrap of paper and this-here bit of charcoal," Henry said, withdrawing them from the pocket of his bib overalls, "and write us a little stick-up note. Then you're gonna hand it over to the bank teller. He's liable to be so scared he'll wet hisself."

"I see," Archie said, relieved to understand how urine was involved.

"Pretty Mary's gonna cover you," he said, marking a dot in the dirt where she would stand. "I'm gonna cover the door, and Creepy's gonna keep the horses ready. You other two fellas split up to watch for trouble. Everybody got that?" Henry said.

There were nods and grunts of assent. Pretty Mary only stared at Archie.

Archie took the paper and charcoal from Henry, and saw in them another opportunity. He printed, in great block letters:

HELP ME. I AM BEING HELD PRISONER BY THIS BAND OF OUTLAWS. THEY WISH TO ROB THIS BANK. I DO NOT. IF YOU HAVE A GUN, PLEASE SHOOT THE MAN GUARDING THE DOOR.

Then he felt Henry breathing over his shoulder. "I think that's about long enough. We want to rob 'em, not give 'em a bedtime story to read. You ought to know that, bein' the lootin'est, and all."

"Ah, yes, quite right, I agree," Archie said, folding the note and putting it in his own pocket.

"How about a little music to pass the time until we go?" Creepy said. "Only this time, how's about a little real music. Do you know 'Old Dan Tucker' or 'Buffalo Gals' ?"

It did not take long for Archie to learn the songs, and they sang along with him, though it was a ho-hum effort at best. When it was time to saddle up, Archie tucked his lute back in its case, slung it over his shoulder, and mounted his horse with the sick twist of dread in his guts. He wondered what the bank teller would do, and if there was any help left for him in this world.

The desperadoes took up their stations at the bank. Archie, his heart pounding so hard he could feel it in his fingertips, waited in line to see the teller. His lute felt like it weighed a hundred pounds.

The man ahead of him in line finished his business and stepped away. Archie tried to gulp, but his mouth was too dry. He took the smudged and folded paper out of his pocket and took a step forward.

"Hello, how can I help you?" the teller said. He looked much the same way bank tellers in London looked: plump, balding, soft about the middle. The thought that this appearance might be a job requirement shot through Archie's mind like a deranged meteor.

"Yes, hello," Archie croaked, and passed the note across the counter. The bank teller took it, read it, then looked back at Archie's face with round confused eyes.

"Is this some kind of a joke?" the teller said.

"If only it were. Robbing banks is a capital crime, right?"

"I don't understand," the teller said.

Henry, nervous to begin with, decided he'd had enough. He took out his mauled shotgun. "What the dern heck don't you understand about 'Hand over the money now,' ya idiot?" he said from the door.

That was when all the bank patrons began to scream and run for the exit. Pretty Mary fired a single shot into the bank's ceiling, causing a great puff of dust to fall into her hair.

"All right, everybody down on the floor!" Henry said. "Archie, I thought you knew what you was doing!"

"Oh, I quite assure you, I–" he began, and that was all he had time to say before Pretty Mary, true to her word, made her move.

She tackled Henry and shouted, "Run for it, Archie!"

Henry, taken off guard by an attack from this quarter, hit the floor in exactly the same way that a feather pillow doesn't.

Archie had forgotten Pretty Mary's promise, but he saw his opportunity, yet another in this great land of them, and ran for the door with Pretty Mary hot on his heels. Henry, none the worse for wear, sat up and turned his cut-down shotgun on the fleeing figures and squeezed first one trigger and then the next.

The first shot hit Pretty Mary in the back. She fell to the dust with a sound like a startled duck, "Ack!"

"That'll teach you to backstab me, you twit!" Henry shouted, and fired again. The second shot, meant to do the same to Archie, went a little high. Archie's lute saved his life, taking about half of the shotgun's blast with a horrid twang. The rest struck Archie's backside. He did not let the pain stop him, though. He grabbed a horse and swung into its saddle. One of the other bank robbers, thinking it was getaway time, jumped on his horse and headed for the hills. The other one had a knife in one hand and a gun in the other, and looked as if he didn't know whether to shoot up the alley or cut across to the other side of town.

As soon as he was sure no one was chasing him, Archie stopped and asked directions to the nearest doctor's office. His poor outraged derriere had taken more than enough abuse and was going on strike.

The doctor had Archie bare his bottom, which he disinfected with iodine. He called for his nurse to come hold the porcelain dish. When she didn't come right away, he hollered again. Archie could see that he was a doctor with no patience.

When the nurse finally came in the room, Archie groaned. It was none other than the blushing girl with the figure of an umbrella, whom he'd met on the stagecoach into town.

The doctor took his tweezers and began plucking out pellets. With each *plink* of a pellet into the dish, the pain in Archie's outraged bottom got worse. He thought with despair about all the long rides and hard seats ahead of him, and how

Western Games
Will Morton

Them Indians chased us a bit,
Us cowboys refusin' to quit
Their warpathin' game,
But I'm downright ashamed,
They Tagged us, and now we are It.

The Last True Gunslinger
Y. B. Cats

Gunslinger Red Bandana stepped into the street, accompanied by the *ting-ting* from his spurs, and a dry desert wind. Sunset orange tinted the town's storefronts, softened their angles, and dressed them in romantic lore. Alas, Rio de Roja shunned wild-western romance in favor of blood and glory, and every respectable townsperson would choose to witness a gunslinger felled by bullets over a happy sunset. This proved true even now, as Red watched townsfolk scramble to find cover with a good view into the street.

"I'm gonna make sure everyone sees yer ugly face, Red! I bet, under that bandana, you're so ugly even yer mama won't stand fer it!" Gummy McGee cawed from street's end. He twirled his pistols – slick, flashy silvers – and dropped them back in their holsters. Rio de Roja's undertaker fancied himself a poet, and Red pictured Gummy's tombstone:

Here lies Gummy, who picked a fight with Red Bandana, because he was a dummy.

It wasn't going to be quite that simple. The sun glared as it slipped behind the western horizon, a squint didn't help, and Gummy stood at the street end with the sun at his back.

Here lies Red Bandana, done in because he couldn't see, the fool before him, Gummy McGee.

"Red." A water barrel in Red's peripheral vision, or someone cowered behind it, tried to get his attention. "Before you git mad, I just want you to know, I have 'em right here."

"You have what, right where, Justus?"

"The bullets," Justus replied. "The bullets I forgot to put back in yer gun, like Susanna told me, after I cleaned it." Red Bandana didn't sweat at gunfights. His veins were icy rivers; he didn't taunt, he didn't gloat, he drew his pistol faster than any man in the west, and everyone knew it. At his brother's confession, however, a hot itch tickled his armpits.

"Which gun," Red said, low. There were several spectators who could throw the fight for a wager's sake.

"I don't remember," was the inevitable answer.

Here lies Justus, kicked in the head by his father's mule, doomed forever after as a fool.

"How many bullets do you have?"

"I have six, Red." Red knew Justus squatted behind the barrel and counted the bullets in his moist palm, over and over. If he drew both six-shooters, their individual weight could reveal which one promised lead venom, and which one didn't. Whenever he fired both guns at once, however, his aim wasn't perfect, and with the glare…

"Git ready to die, you ugly son-of-a–" McGee stopped short. Red took a step toward him, hands poised above his shooters. "What're you doing?"

"You want to see my ugly face?" A surprised murmur rose from the hidden crowd. McGee twitched his trigger fingers as Red continued a slow approach.

"Why would I wanna see it now? I'll see yer face when you're dead." McGee spat tobacco to the dirt, and juice ran over his chin. Gummy missed more teeth than the ones he had left. Red's toes touched McGee's cowboy-hat shadow, and stopped.

"It'll make you famous."

"I could kill you with my eyes closed from here," McGee chortled. Behind him the sun dipped below the horizon, and released the sky from its glare. Red eased his left hand up and hooked his forefinger on the bandana's edge at his cheek. His right hand slid its pistol from its holster while McGee stood, transfixed. Red's right pistol felt heavy – but heavy enough?

"Ready?" Red asked, and McGee sneered. Red eased the bandana down and revealed… fair, beardless skin and soft, red lips.

"You're a–" McGee's eyes widened, and Red's trigger finger took the chance.

Click.

Red looked down at his pistol as McGee did the same. Both looked back to the other; Red shrugged, and McGee snickered.

"Nobody's gonna believe–" Gummy began, and made his move; whipped his pistol up in a one-hand grab. Red's left hand flew to its pistol and raised it in a flash.

Bang.

The gunslingers lingered, coiled and frozen in place. Brown and red drool oozed from Gummy's mouth, and he lurched forward. His hands clawed the air for Red's bandana and meant to tear it loose. Red caught his hands; Gummy leered and groped Red's chest. He smeared his drool across Red's front as he slid to the ground. Red struggled to maintain composure; Red Bandana wouldn't shoot this man in the face after he fell... but Susanna, the sharp-tongued saloon girl, would.

"Red Bandana... is a woman." Gummy's boot heels kicked divots in the dirt as his lips quivered their final words. Red didn't think anyone was close enough to hear, and tugged the bandana back to where it belonged. Someone whistled the all-clear signal, and Rio de Roja's citizenry erupted into the street. Amid cheers and slaps on the back Red saw Justus make his way near, head bent in concentration over his palm.

"Here are yer bullets, Red. I didn't lose 'em."

"Thanks, Justus." Red received the wayward bullets, and Justus turned to snatch money shoved in his direction. By the look of it, quite a few people thought Gummy would win.

Red considered his dark-silver pistols, with their etched snakes curled around the barrels. He opened the right pistol and found four bullets. He opened the left pistol and found... one. That meant Justus loaded four bullets in one pistol and two in the other. A madman, fool or the devil incarnate would do such a thing, and Red realized given the odds, Gummy McGee should be alive. Red looked at Gummy's boots – visible among the crowd's feet – and watched the boots recede as the undertaker dragged Gummy from view. Red shuddered at the sight.

"Justus, I'm headed fer the saloon, and up to see Susanna."

"Ok, Red. I'll make sure nobody disturbs."

Red swung the saloon doors inward and stepped into

Halfway Saloon's lioness den, where long-legged entertainers were known across the west for their humor, card playing, and… other talents. A few cattle hands turned an eye at Red's entrance, but most remained enthralled by rosy cheeks, red lips, and heady perfume. A stampede couldn't draw a man from Halfway Saloon's amorous embrace, and that was just fine with Red, who found it easy to disappear in the smoke, music, and laughter.

Susanna hunched on her elbows over a short whiskey. She stared hard at the amber liquid, swirled the glass, and tilted her head back to down its contents. This was not what she had in mind when, not long ago, she yearned for adventure. She wanted to travel, and see the world. So far, she'd set foot in countless western towns – hardly an admirable feat.

If she had one wish she'd wish Red Bandana, the real Red Bandana, never tried to impress her with a stupid pistol trick. *Let's step outside,* he said, *and I'll show you my trick.* It turned out a dark alley, a pistol twirl, and errant shot were all it took to interrupt Red Bandana's infamous persona.

What did she do then? Did she run far and fast, like any sensible girl would? No, she rolled Red to his side for a better look. *¡Asesina! You killed him!* A short man in preacher's garb stepped from the shadows. *I didn't! I didn't kill him!* She protested even though she knew her words were worthless. The Padre said: *I'll keep this secret, if Red Bandana lives on in service to La Casa de Dios.*

A dime novel fell at her elbow on the bar as her least-favorite short man sat too close for comfort. The novel's cover depicted a bandana-masked gunslinger, triumphant over a slain opponent. The ornate-lettered title read: *Adventures of Red Bandana, the Last True Gunslinger.* Padre Domingo leaned into her vision's edge.

"I bought this today at the corner *tienda*," he whispered. Few patrons remained in the saloon at so late an hour and most dozed on their tables. Padre Domingo, however, spoke in a hushed voice and glanced over his shoulder.

"I don't think Red's that tall or lean," Susanna said into her glass, and tossed it back. She balanced on the stool's peg supports and leaned over to pull a whiskey bottle from behind the bar. She poured herself another shallow glass. "Pour you a drink?" The Padre glared, not amused. Susanna shrugged. "I overheard Red say he retired today, Padre."

"*¿Es verdad?*" Padre Domingo lifted an eyebrow. Susanna nodded and winced at the familiar whiskey burn in her throat.

"Do you think Red's secret is safe in retirement? Many heroes grow in fame when they retire, and it would be such a shame for Red to be exposed as an *impostora…* and worse."

"I'm more afraid of a pine box than Red is afraid of exposure. Besides, who'll believe you?"

"It's your word against mine, and I'd say you threatened to kill me if I told, after I witnessed you kill the real Red Bandana in cold blood. And, of course, there is Justus to consider." Susanna regarded the Padre with renewed contempt. "There's no telling what the knowledge his brother died some time ago would do to him." Their deal cinched her neck, and she touched her throat with a distracted hand.

"Red Bandana will be shot dead someday. What will you do then?"

"When that occurs, I assure you, you will no longer care what happens on this earthly plain. God will show your filthy soul no mercy. You should pray, when that day dawns, Justus becomes blind and deaf." Susanna emptied her glass, and returned it with a slam to the bar's blemished surface. "Of course, a tithing may help you regain the Lord's favor…?" The Padre leaned even closer and displayed his hand, palm up.

Susanna stifled her anger, and moved to where Justus slumbered on a table, his cheek drool-glued to its surface. She searched his pockets and found meager leftovers; paper money she crumpled further and slapped into the Padre's limp grasp.

Sometime later, Susanna lifted her head from the bar, and opened bleary eyes. A tall man, dressed in black, tugged his hat's brim.

"Pardon, Ma'am. I couldn't help but notice you seem distressed."

"I'm no damsel, cowpoke. Rescue somebody else."

"Are you in need of a rescue?"

"No – yes, I'd be obliged if you knew how to undo a deal with *El Diablo*. Otherwise, leave me be before I retch all over yer fancy, black boots." The stranger seemed amused.

"My boots would be honored to receive the stomach contents of such a beauty," he smiled.

"Then, have a seat Mister–"

"Bart, you can call me Bart." He sat on the next stool over. "Quite a fight today, wouldn't you say? I saw the whole thing; quite a show."

"I reckon so." Susanna pushed the whiskey bottle away; as far as she could reach. She swore she'd never drink again. Bart picked up the dime novel Padre Domingo left behind, and thumbed its pages.

"So, you made a deal with the devil?"

"I traded a hangman's noose fer a leash, fortune, and fame."

"Fame? Beg your pardon, but I've never heard of you, Miss–"

"Susanna, and of course you haven't heard of me. I'm just shootin' my mouth off. Would you like a drink? I'm the barkeep, but I work from this side of the bar, so I git better tips."

"Ah no, thank you. I'm here to find my old friend – Red Bandana." Bart's dark eyes searched hers, and Susanna felt heat rise to her face. "But, the one I saw today couldn't be my old friend. Every gunslinger's style is unique, and the Red I knew was… showy. The one I saw today was cold, measured… and more petite in stature." Did he know? Had he guessed? It seemed so, but what did that mean? "Red definitely didn't wear lipstick, either." By God, he knew – he must've seen when she lowered the bandana.

"What would you do if you knew the real Red was dead?" Susanna avoided his gaze and picked at a scratch on the bar.

"I'd be very disappointed. Red owes me a gunfight, and I'm here to collect."

"You call him an old friend, and you want to shoot at him?"

"Yes – may I count on your discretion? You may've heard of Black Bart?" Susanna's eyes widened at the name, but she tried not to look too impressed.

"Black Bart: the gentleman bandit and poet? I've heard."

"Well, here I am. Years ago Red and I made a deal – when I felt the law over my shoulder, Black Bart and Red Bandana would fight, and... Bart would lose."

"Lose, you mean, die?" Susanna's eyebrows rose. Black Bart tilted his head and gave her a sly smile.

"That's what everyone was supposed to think," he winked. "I always knew I'd miss the life, after I gave it up. On the other hand, I'd like to stay loose from the noose a while longer, so now I don't know what to do. Rather, I wouldn't know what to do, if I knew Red was dead."

"Black Bart!" Justus stumbled into the bar between them. "I wondered when we'd see you again! You've met Susanna; Red's girl?" Bart leaned around Justus and touched his hat's brim again. "Susanna," Justus aimed his wretched breath at her, "where's Red – go get him. He'll want to see Bart–"

"He's sleeping, Justus, and doesn't want to be disturbed."

"Well, we'll just wait fer him then." Justus plopped on the stool between them and put his head down on the bar. In a moment, he snored with abandon.

"Bart," Susanna rose and rested her hand on Justus's shoulder, "I have a proposition fer you." Bart's eyebrows rose in mock surprise. "Not that kind of proposition, Mr. Gentleman Bandit; one more likely to solve all our problems."

Dawn's pale shades lit the sky, and Rio de Roja's main street lingered in quiet. From the farthest end, a small figure appeared and ran down the street at a break-neck pace.

"Wake up! Wake up! Red Bandana and Black Bart are gonna fight!" A small boy hollered and paused for a breath before he kept on. "Wake up, or you'll miss the greatest gunfight in history!" Shades snapped up windows while front doors swung open, and citizens in their nightcaps emerged with sleepy steps. Black Bart descended from the saloon, head-to-toe in black, with a new addition to his attire. Citizens whispered to each other as he passed.

"Is that Black Bart? I didn't know he was so short. Have you seen him before?"

"Nah, but look at him with that black bandana up over his face; he must think he can rattle Red's nerves."

The saloon's doors swung open and Red Bandana stepped forward; he nodded at Bart and made his way up the street. Black Bart checked both pistols while he waited, and then eased them down in their holsters. When Red reached a hundred paces, he turned. Black Bart crouched into a gunslinger's stance, and waited.

Silence settled in, and even the desert wind held its breath until: *B-bang!* Both gunslingers moved so fast, few saw their hands move at all. Black Bart swayed, fell forward, and landed in the dirt, and those who watched him gasped at the sight. Red Bandana crossed the distance to Black Bart's body.

"Listen to me, citizens of Rio de Roja. Black Bart was a gentleman, and a friend. We will treat his body with the utmost care. Where is the undertaker?" The grizzled undertaker distinguished himself from the crowd. "Bart left with me special instructions for his burial, which we will follow, exact. Bart wanted these words on his tombstone; I hope you can fit it all in." Red pulled a crumpled paper from his pocket and handed it to the undertaker. The undertaker glanced at it, nodded, grabbed Bart's boot, and drug him away. Numerous citizens asked what the note contained.

"I will tell you, good people," Red said, and began to recite a rhyme. Padre Domingo watched from a doorway, and stepped forward. He opened his mouth; Red caught his eye, and tapped a pistol with a finger.

"Red!" Justus stumbled from the saloon, and almost toppled at Red's feet. "I missed a fight? Did you win?"

"Indeed I did." Red guided Justus back toward the saloon.

"I don't know how you can shoot someone before breakfast," Justus frowned.

"You're right. I should get something to eat."

"Red, you sound different."

"I do?"

"More like yer old self!" Justus laughed. "Where's Bart?"

"He'll be along. Listen, Susanna's gone, but Bart's going to be with us from now on. The law's after him, so keep it quiet."

"Okay Red. I never liked Susanna anyway."

"Oh?"

"Yeah, she's too fussy. You need a woman who's not afraid to get a little dirt under her fingernails."

The townsfolk didn't bother to attend Black Bart's burial, since they already knew what was on his tombstone. When the undertaker filled a hole up with dirt, no one was there to ask why there wasn't a coffin, or a body. Atop the dirt pile the undertaker positioned a tombstone that should've been larger:

*Black Bart**

I've labored long and hard for bread,
For honor, and for riches,
But on my corns too long you've tread,
You fine-haired sons of b.

* Note: The poem is credited to Charles Earl Bolles, or Black Bart, (1829-Disappeared). It was left at the scene of a stagecoach robbery in 1877.

HORSEFEATHERS
Will Morton

In a canyon we found 'em at dusk,
Two rustlers who put up a fuss.
"Jes' a mis-un'erstandin',
We ain't caught red-handed,
These hosses o' yourn, they stoled us!"

LOOPY PROBLEM
Will Morton

I bought me a rope, and the fact is,
I'm needin' a little more practice,
'Cos I tried for some cows,
They was big as a house,
But I missed 'em and lassoed a cactus.

COWBOY GEOMETRY
Will Morton

Now Jeb was a thinkin' ol' wrangler,
"Our round-up sure fills me with anger.
This corral ain't no circle,
I re-name this work fer
A square-up, or mebbe rectangler."

PAPER LIES
Colin P. Davies

Johnny Mephisto was a boy out of time, an anachronism, a tick of a backwards tock. While his peers filled their days with specious spectacle and synesthetic thrills, Johnny read novels. While his classmates studied astrogation and alien anatomy, indulged in exotic stimulation and flits to the moon, Johnny rode the purple sage. Not for Johnny the crystal towers and orbital elevators of 2089. No, he preferred his chamber, an armchair, and Max Brand.

Professor Strict, feeling somewhat guilty for introducing the student to the dusty pleasures of the college library, determined to cure the lad of his romantic illusions. This could best be achieved by first establishing a rapport—that is, *it takes an outlaw to catch an outlaw*—so he strapped on a sidearm, marched stiffly to Johnny's room, and knocked three times on the freshly-chalked sign *Mephisto Gulch*.

The door slid to the side.

He found the sixteen year old student smoking a cigarette, wearing a cowboy hat, and reading a book. The professor coughed and wafted a hand through the trails of smoke.

With a finger, Johnny raised the brim of his hat and examined his visitor.

"You 'n me need to talk... Pardner," Strict drawled. "Seems like I ain't seen you in town for...." His voice trailed off as Johnny produced a colt and aimed it at the octogenarian's heart.

"You're mighty brave showing your face round these here parts...*old timer*."

The professor flicked back his lab coat. "I'm carrying heat."

Johnny scowled and slipped his colt back into his belt. "Wrong genre, Professor."

"Oh...." Strict sat on the edge of the bed. "Johnny... I'm a little concerned about your studies. You've been skipping lessons and you missed your jaunt into orbit."

"I don't like heights."

"And you're smoking a cigarette."

"And drinking….." Johnny hoisted a bottle of whiskey. "I'm in character for the period."

"This is the *twenty-first* century. I really can't allow…."

Johnny was reading again.

"This obsession is unhealthy. I'm duty bound to help you."

Johnny turned the page.

Strict's voice took on a softer tone: "I can show you how it really was."

Johnny bookmarked and closed the book. The professor had his attention.

"I propose to send you on a field trip... back to the *real* Wild West."

Johnny stared at his teacher, eyes round as silver dollars.

"Don't you have anything to say?" asked Strict.

A smile split Johnny's face. "Yee-ha!"

Johnny knew the cow was landing the moment he felt the thudding of hooves on the ground. It could not have come at a more welcome time—the blind pressure of warm flesh in his face had set his skin sweating. He turned his head ready for the escape. His throat was dry and desperate—he hoped Kayleigh was waiting with the canteen.

They stopped.

Johnny released his grip on the loose folds of skin and pushed. He squelched out of the kanga-cow's pouch like a new-born joey and dropped to his knees. It was only now in the heavenly scent of grass and lavender that he became aware of the animal stench in his nostrils. He took a kerchief from his pocket, wiped his face, cleared his nose, and looked up. The brilliance of the high Arizona sun was muted to beige by the huge hydrogen bladder which extended up from the back of the creature.

He stood and patted the flyer's hairy flank in a gesture of congratulation. They had cleared the top of the mesquite tree—possibly thirty feet—before Johnny's weight had become too much for the cow.

"Johnny!"

He turned. Kayleigh was running towards him. She tossed the canteen. He grasped for it, but her throw was way off. The bottle bounced on the dry grass and came to rest within an inch of a pool of putrid dung. Johnny bit his tongue on an outburst; he didn't want Kayleigh weeping again. He'd only known her for seven days—since he'd tumbled down the years to materialise upon a Queen Anne chair at a polished wood table in a palatial dining room—but he'd come to like the neurotic little elf. "So what do you reckon?" he asked. "Can we reach the top of the tower?"

"I'd say so," the cow told him. "Even better if you could shed a little weight."

"If I was any thinner the wind could carry me like a tumbleweed." Johnny retrieved the canteen, drank, and screwed back the top. "Let's have more enthusiasm and less criticism." He handed the canteen to Kayleigh.

She laughed. "Between you and me, maybe it would be easier if we trapped and tortured Doctor Frankenstone to find out what's up there."

"*Between you and me?*" the cow mimicked. "Am I not here?"

Kayleigh ignored the animal. "I'd love to repay him for yanking me out of my world, away from my parents." She sniffed, and Johnny thought she was going to lose it again.

"At least you knew yours," he said. "Anyway, I'm here to find the real West, not battle sorcerers."

"I used to be a real cow," the hybrid told no-one in particular.

Johnny read disappointment in Kayleigh's face. But this wasn't only about revenge; she wanted the old mage to reveal the secret of his power, the secret she believed he hid in the wooden cabin perched at the top of a forty foot pole. Johnny was not interested in power, but he did suspect that what he was looking for was up there—it was the only place he hadn't looked. He stooped to bring his face closer to hers. "I was sent here to learn…and the Doctor has been kind to me, considering I'm an uninvited guest."

"Okay!" she said, and she flicked Johnny's soft brown hair.

"Mooooo," said the kanga-cow. "See…I can still do it."

145

Kayleigh skipped and twirled so that her golden hair fanned out to reveal the cute pointed peaks of her ears. She gave him a smile. "And what have you learned so far, Johnny-boy?"

A weariness came over Johnny and he started down the path towards the ranch, then shouted back: "I've learned that professors can *not* be trusted."

The dining room was a marvel. From outside, the house showed the fading timber of the traditional homestead and, inside, the house was basic and barely-comfortable; but this room was classic luxury. Royalty could eat here. A thick crimson carpet was a festival for the feet and the two chandeliers were like frozen white fireworks. Fine artworks hung upon wood panel walls. Thanks to an attentive eye in art class, Johnny recognised Hogarth's *The Stage Coach* and *The Enraged Musician*. Against the wall stood a piano, which the Doctor would play on occasion—*play* being a rather generous appellation for the atonal aural assault generated by his frustrated fingers. Frankenstone had confessed to a taste for the finer things, but so far had managed to furnish just the one room.

Arsenic the Cook had prepared a meal of turnip, dried fish, bean soup and bread, and Johnny, Kayleigh, Mutant and the mage tucked in. Conversation was muted. Cutlery clattered. Mutant slurped. Doctor Frankenstone bit both his turnip and his lip. When he could hold back no longer, he said, "King Cactus uprooted overnight and has replanted himself still closer. He resists all my attack spells and shoots spines if I approach. My life's work is at risk."

Mutant peered over the rim of his raised bowl.

Kayleigh's face was impassive. "That's too bad, I suppose."

Johnny sipped sullenly. This wasn't where he was supposed to be. These weren't the people he'd expected to meet. They didn't even talk right!

"Johnny…" said Frankenstone. "I saw you jumping today. May I ask why?"

Johnny was ripping up bread with his teeth, so Kayleigh spoke for him. "I showed him the jumping game, but he needs to get over his vertigo and climb into the kanga-cow's pouch feet first, not head first."

"I don't like heights," Johnny mumbled.

Kayleigh sneered.

"Give me a few more days," Johnny told her, "and I'll be able to jump as high as the…as high as *you* can."

Doctor Frankenstone sat back in his chair. "Let's hope King Cactus gives us a couple more days." He sipped at his coffee and examined his lanky young visitor. "Johnny…tell me more about why you came here. I love your tales of 'wagon-trains' and 'rail-roads' and—he sniggered— 'cow-boys'."

"Well that's what I was expecting to find here…not an eccentric sorcerer and his weird retinue and no other soul for a thousand square miles of dry wilderness."

"Eccentric? I could take offence."

"In the Old West, that would lead to a duel, a fight, *one on one,* and only one can be the one to survive."

"That sounds confusing," said the Doctor through a mouthful of food.

"It's amazingly simple. A matter of honor."

"A man's gotta do what a man's gotta do!" Frankenstone spluttered with laughter, spraying chewed turnip across the table.

Johnny scowled.

"Tell me more." The sorcerer composed himself, while Kayleigh wiped the table. "Tell me everything."

Johnny had to admit to some sympathy for King Cactus. The one-time apprentice of the sorcerer had hoped to elope with a substantial portion of Frankenstone's wealth, but he'd been trapped, sliced, divided, blended and combined and eventually planted outside in the vegetable garden—a man/cactus hybrid— to grow quietly and dwell on his humiliation. A just fate, so the Doctor had decided, for a man with such a stupid name.

But King Cactus had pulled up his roots and fled, to grow taller, wider and stronger in the hidden hills. And now he was back.

Nothing would stop him from destroying Frankenstone's *Tower of Power* and, with luck, the cruel sorcerer himself.

Night fell like a door slamming. Johnny hid behind the water tank and watched as Frankenstone approached the mysterious tower. Not far away, a black space in the stars revealed where King Cactus loomed.

Same as every evening, the sorcerer placed his palms on the pole and ascended swiftly, pulling himself onto the narrow balcony and thus admitting himself into the cabin. Johnny had tried to mimic the mage, but the pole refused to hoist him—hence his jumping practice.

Johnny slipped back into the kitchen to find Kayleigh plaiting Mutant's tentacles. "I need to talk," he said.

Mutant turned a bloodshot eye in his direction.

"To Kayleigh…."

Mutant slithered away to his kennel.

Johnny took the elf-girl by the arm. "It's got to be tomorrow. Another day and King Cactus may topple the tower… and then I'll never know the truth about the real West."

"And when you do find out…what then?"

"*Then* I suppose I'll be taken home."

Tears glistened in her huge green eyes. "I thought that we'd always be friends."

Johnny felt a hardening in his throat. He didn't make friends easily and would be sad to say goodbye to Kayleigh, but what could he do? It seemed he was as trapped to follow his plot as any character in a book.

But didn't characters live forever in memories?

"We will," he said. "*We will!*"

Johnny rose before the sun, chased Kayleigh out of bed, and they headed for the fields. Kanga-cow had been expecting them and had breakfasted sufficient to generate maximum lift. Morning dew glistened on the inflated hydrogen bladder as the sun crested the ragged hills.

The tower cast a long shadow from the house to their feet and Johnny followed this path back towards his destiny.

As they approached the tower, they entered a second shadow; King Cactus was now so close to the house that Johnny could smell a hateful acridity on the air, as though Evil itself had a scent—somewhere between an infected wound and mouldy cheese.

Close to the foot of the tower, Johnny patted the kangacow's side. "Are you ready?"

"One belch and we're airborne."

Johnny slipped one leg, then the other, into the cow's pouch. He wriggled around until his shoulders and head peeked clear of the hide.

Kayleigh laughed. "Right way up this time? Very brave."

"I may cover my eyes."

She reached forward and touched his hand. "Take care."

There was a throaty groan as gas was released into the bladder and the creature rose into the air.

Despite the worrying chill in his stomach, Johnny kept his eyes upon the pole.

They rose with increasing speed and he began to fret that they would miss their target; but as the bulk of the cabin loomed, the cow snapped its teeth upon the balcony rail and they came to a halt.

Johnny reached forward for the rail, but found it too far away. He eased himself out of the pouch, averting his gaze from the ground, and stretched out a hand. No…still out of reach.

Summoning all his courage—his very own High Noon moment— Johnny grabbed fistfuls of the cow's underbelly and lunged for the rail.

"Ouch," the cow told him, through clamped teeth.

Johnny hauled himself onto the wooden balcony. "Sorry."

He took a glance down and saw Kayleigh waving with excitement. He gave a wave in return. "King Cactus is moving!" she screamed. "*Towards you!*"

"There's no going back now!" he replied.

Ahead of him was the door to the truth. Would he be able to handle the truth? Of course he would.

He turned the doorknob and walked in.

Sat either side of a desk were two identical old men who looked up as he entered. Each possessed wispy white hair

149

and an unkempt beard. They wore small round spectacles and exuded the air of scholars. The desk between them was strewn with papers and pictures, pens and paints. A typewriter sat in front of each man.

Johnny glanced at the walls. Apart from the single window, the surfaces were covered with posters, sheets of paper, notes and images. A Spanish guitar was propped in the corner.

"All this," he said. "What is it? And who are you?"

One of the old men smiled. "Tweedledim...."

"...and Tweedledum."

"We invent...."

"...and create."

"We write...."

"...and draw."

"We make new...."

"...and make real."

"Composer...."

"...constructor."

"Impressario...."

"...incommunicado."

Johnny stepped up to the desk and shuffled through the papers. Here were stories: Billy the Kid, Buffalo Bill, Custer's Last Stand; Posters: wanted dead or alive; Paintings: Sitting Bull, the coming of the railroad.... "You're creating the Wild West?" This was crazy! Could the Wild West have been built here; a mythic jigsaw born of the imagination of two fraternal freaks? "Paper lies!" Johnny yelled and shoved papers from the desk. A deception wrapped up in time.

"All fiction is...."

"...paper lies."

The cabin shook violently. Walls creaked, more papers flew to the floor.

King Cactus was attacking the pole.

Johnny rushed out onto the balcony. Kanga-cow, still hanging onto the rail, winked at him. Johnny peered over as far as he dared, but could not see to the rear.

He reached forward to pull the cow, and the pouch, closer, but the tower shook again and the creature lost its grip. It began to fall.

King Cactus must have seen this as an attack, for he fired

150

several spines into the fragile bladder. With a POP, gas gushed and the cow tore off into the sky, whirling like a burst balloon.

The tower shook again and Johnny heard a cracking sound. The pole would not last much longer.

At that moment, Doctor Frankenstone came rushing out of the house only to dash back inside pursued by a posse of spines.

The air trembled with laughter; a malicious vegetable voice that shook the pole and stirred the dirt and...was cut short as the airborne kanga-cow, either through a heroic feat of willpower, or simply the laws of gravity, irony, and poetic justice, came hurtling back to earth to smash into King Cactus. Pieces of luxuriant green flesh showered in all directions as the bursting, disintegrating plant broke the cow's fall.

Johnny was saved; the tower was saved; the West was saved.

As he turned to give the old scholars the good news, Johnny found them standing beside him.

"Good...."

"...bye."

They shoved and, screaming, he pivoted over the rail and fell into his future.

Professor Strict hurried to Johnny's chamber. Now that the boy had had days to absorb the lesson of the field trip, it was time to reinforce the necessity of cooperation and to receive his deserved plaudits.

He found Johnny sitting in his armchair, wearing a wide-brimmed hat, and reading.

Strict could hardly get his words out. "I...I thought the lesson would be clear... unmistakeable... unavoidable."

Johnny looked up from his book, his young face hidden behind a white beard and glasses. "Which lesson would that be, Professor?"

For a moment, Strict was stunned. "I showed you the Old West... the *Real West*."

"You showed me somewhere else, a *fantasy*."

"*Exactly!*" The professor nodded vigorously. "Yes, a

fantasy. The whole mythology is a fantasy. I hoped to hammer that lesson home and kill this obsession with westerns."

"Your lesson was most impressive, Professor, and very effective."

A modicum of pride returned to Strict and he threw back his shoulders. "How is it then that I find you still reading?"

"Tell me, Professor...." Johnny beamed and held out his garishly-colored book. "Have you ever heard of Terry Pratchett?"

COWPOKE NAMED TEX
John Smith

A latter-day cowpoke named Tex
Rode his horse through the whole Metroplex.
He occasioned much mirth
In Big D and Fort Worth
And more than a few auto wrecks.

THE SILLIEST AUTHORS IN THE WEST

Aaron Polson was born on the Ides of March: a good day for him, unlucky for Julius Caesar. He currently lives in Lawrence, Kansas with his wife, two sons, and a tattooed rabbit. To pay the bills, Aaron attempts to teach high school students the difference between irony and coincidence. His stories have featured magic goldfish, monstrous beetles, and even a book of lullabies for baby vampires. You can visit him on the web at www.aaronpolson.com.

Adrienne Lockhart spends her free time writing, traveling, and reveling in all around silliness. Her great goals in life are to continue publishing, see the world, and one day manage to cook an entirely edible meal (the latter, at this rate, seeming an unlikely goal to be reached in this lifetime).

Alex Moisi spends most of is time trying to rob stage coaches so he can keep funding his addiction to Amazon.com. For updates on his adventures check out his infrequently updated blog at dracken.co.nr

Aurelio Rico Lopez III hails from the Philippines where they have neither indians nor cowboys. When he was a kid, Aurelio's family owned a small farm, along with a mare, a dozen cows, and a mean-tempered water buffalo. Presently, Aurelio drives a car. It's faster and makes less of a mess.

Beth Lynn Clegg, Houston, began writing at almost seventy. To her amazement, she's been published in a variety of genre. She also enjoys church activities, gardening, her children, grandchildren, friends, and a spoiled-rotten cat. She is a member of The Writers' League of Texas.

Christine Rains is a tale-tellin' gal living with her husband in southern Indiana. When not spinning stories, she likes to bury herself in a good book and travel. She has too many college degrees and six short stories published. Please visit her website at http://christinerains.net/.

Colin P. Davies is a Building Surveyor from Liverpool, England, and has been writing fiction since the last century. His stories have appeared in numerous magazines, including Paradox and Asimov's and have made the Locus Recommended Reading List and the British Science Fiction Association Award nominations, as well as gaining two Honorable Mentions in The Year's Best SF. His story "The Defenders" was in The Year's Best SF #22, edited by Gardner Dozois. His first collection "Tall Tales on the Iron Horse" was published in 2008 by Bewildering Press.His website is www.colinpdavies.com

Dal Jeanis is the only one in his family not born in Texas. He was a lonely hybrid - California boy with Texas roots - until he came out to Dallas for a visit and met the lady who taught him that the roots were the most important part of the plant. Married to her since 1997, now Dal writes all manner of strange hybrid stuff, like long suffering Billy Steadman's continuing saga of a Western life with the dragon, **Goose**

Danny Birt is a science fiction and fantasy author, filker, composer, music therapist, and massage therapist. His fantasy series "The Laurian Pentology" is currently halfway through being published by Cyberwizard Productions, starting with the book "Ending an Ending." For more information on Danny and his works, visit www.DannyBirt.com

Derringer Award winning author **Earl Staggs** has seen many of his short stories published in magazines and anthologies. He served as Managing Editor of Futures Mystery Anthology Magazine and as President of the Short Mystery Fiction Society. His novel MEMORY OF A MURDER earned twelve Five Star reviews online at Amazon and B&N. His column "Write Tight" appears in Apollo's Lyre at http://apollos-lyre.tripod.com/ and he is a member of Make Mine Mystery at http://makeminemystery.blogspot.com/ He welcomes comments on his work at earlstaggs@sbcglobal.net

Gary Every has won several journalism awards for his newspaper columns about the southwest including Apache Naichee Ceremony and Losing Geronimo's Language. His newest book Shadow of the OhshaD is a collection of the best of the columns featuring stagecoach bandtis, prospectors, warriors, soldiers, gunfights and more. OhshaD is a Native American word for jaguar. the book can be purchased by emailing garyevery@gmail.com

Gary R. Hoffman has taught school, been self-employed, and traveled in a motor home. He has published over 200 short stories. www.garyrhoffman.com

H Earl Wilkinson lives in NE Ohio with a spouse, three cats, and a new daughter. Prior publications were placed in Abandoned Towers and Flashing Swords. Apart from fencing and gaming, a space western novel is also in the works.

JH Hobson would like to say that you can find the writings of JH Hobson in just about any publication you can think of. Of course, what JH Hobson would like to say and what JH Hobson can say are...ahem...two different things. Still, you can, if you like, find more work by this inscrutable scribbler in O Sweet Flowery Roses, Diddledog, Champagne Shivers, Appalling Limericks, Garbanzo, Vicious Verse and Revolting Rhyme (Coscom), Lost Innocence (NiteBlade) and many other rather interesting places.

Jax is married and lives in Plymouth, England. He's had 'quite a few' short stories, poems and articles printed in magazines in UK and USA. His ambition is to write novels.

John Weagly has toured the US as a writer/performer with "Authorized Personnel: A Comedy and Improv Team" and has had over 30 plays produced by theaters around the world. He is a Spinetingler Award nominee and Derringer Award winner with over 50 short stories and poems published in a variety of mediums. www.johnweagly.com.

K.C. Ball lives in Seattle, a stone's throw from Puget Sound. She is an active member of the Science Fiction and Fantasy Writers of America. Her poetry and fiction has appeared in print and online in various publications, including Analog, Flash Fiction Online, Big Pulp, Every Day Poets and Murky Depths. Her short story, Coward's Steel, was a 2009 Writers of the Future winner and will appear August 2010 in the Writers of the Future 26 anthology. K.C. blogs at http://kcball.wordpress.com.

Kaysee Renee Robichaud lives and writes in San Antonio, Texas. Please don't prairie dog for her, she doesn't find that particularly endearing. Okay, maybe a little.

Laura Finlay was born in Springhill, Louisiana and spent her formative years in the backwoods and byways of rural Mississippi, Louisiana, and Texas. Her writing reflects her affection for boots, spurs, horses, and of course...cowboys. She currently resides in Denton, Texas and her poems have appeared in THE WYOMING COMPANION, ROPE AND WIRE, and on the cowboypoetry. com website.

Linda Lee Booth is 43 and works for the Hampshire County Council. She has been writing short stories and poems for many years and has a passion for writing. She has had several published and would now like to publish her children's novel.

Lindsey N. Williams was born in Mississippi and grew up in Texas. She began writing stories at age 6 and was first published in 2002. Her most recent publications can be found in "Leaves in the Wind, The Denton Writers League Anthology". She is a piano technician and tuner and lives with her husband and their two children in Krum, Texas.

Lyn McConchie's recent stories have appeared in anthologies and in Abandoned Towers magazines. She had two books out in 2009, a western, SOUTH OF RIO CHAMA, and the fifth (RURAL DAZE AND (K)NIGHTS) in her non-fiction humor series, about her farm and animals - and her YA supernatural fantasy, SUMMER OF DREAMING, appears very shortly from Cyberwizard productions. Lyn's website is lynmcconchie.com

Matthew Baugh has been writing stories for the last five years. He has often combined Westerns with horror and fantasy elements, but this is by far his silliest Western. He hails from the Southwest but currently hangs his spurs in the Chicago area.

Melanie Pearce resides in sunny Swindon, England. Melanie is a working mum and is a writer of children's stories and poems. She lives in a very happy and mad home along with husband Steve, seven year old Jordan and her faithful laptop.

Patricia Wellingham-Jones has a longtime interest in 'healing writing' and the benefits people gain from writing and reading their work together. Her poems, stories and articles are widely published; chapbooks include Don't Turn Away: Poems About Breast Cancer, Voices on the Land, and End-Cycle, poems about caregiving. She believes there is always room in life for humor.

Novelist, blogger, and award winning travel writer, **Perry P. Perkins** is a stay-at-home dad who lives with his wife Victoria and their two-year-old daughter Grace, in the Pacific Northwest. His novels include Just Past Oysterville, Shoalwater Voices, and the outdoor humor collection, "Elk Hunters Don't Cry." Perry has written for hundreds of magazines and anthologies, and his inspirational stories have been included in twelve Chicken Soup collections.

Examples of his published work can be found online at www.perryperkinsbooks.com, and on his Portland Fatherhood Examiner page.

Rob Mancebo has been a soldier, a classified courier, a security technician, and a guard, Currently he is a medical assistant and X-ray technician with an urgent-care facility. He also edits and writes Historical fiction, Horror, Fantasy, SciFi, and Westerns.

A genuine "Okie from Muskogee," **Sarah Ashwood** is a full-time college student working towards a B.A. in English from American Military University. Her short work and poetry have appeared in a variety of publications while her first book, a volume of poetry titled A Minstrel's Musings, was published by Cyberwizard Productions in April 2009. In 2010, Sarah's Young Adult fantasy novel, Knight's Rebirth, will be published by the same. Along with her cousin, Carol Green, Sarah is co-editor of the fantasy ezine, Moon Drenched Fables. For more information, please visit www.sarahashwood.com.

Steve Doyle is an award-winning writer whose poem "Footprints in my Garden", coupled with photography by Maria Touchette, won third prize at a juried art show put on by the Hudson Area Arts Alliance. Some of Steve's other poems have appeared in The Wayfarer's Journal, Residential Aliens and Flashes in the Dark. His poem "A Leprechaun's Tale" appeared in Strange Worlds of Lunacy: The Galaxy's Silliest Anthology available at Lyn Perry's storefront.

RODEO
Will Morton

To the rodeo went cowboy Ross,
An' he come back to us mighty cross.
"I kin ride Brahma bulls,
Or broncs buckin' like fools,
But not my old wood hobby hoss!"

Author, artist, and all-round good egg, **Timothy A. Sayell** has been a lifelong fan of various pulpy genre stories, especially of the fantasy and sci-fi variety. He is also an ardent admirer of good and witty humor, and enjoyed positive but brief experiences as a stand-up comic and comedic stage actor. He currently lives and loses money in beautiful, scenic Las Vegas, Nevada, where he often complains about the lack of rain and maintains a modest website offering more information about his published stories. His website is http://dungeoneer.webs.com/ and all are welcome to visit!

Whitt Pond was born in Texas shortly after a famous UFO sighting, which explains a lot. He has at various times been a Boy Scout, a West Point cadet, an MIT grad, and a Peace Corps voluteer, all part of his clever plan to remain undetected among the earthlings. For some unknown reason, he always lives within walking distance of a really good Chinese restaurant.

Born in West Virginia, **Will Morton** now lives in the Los Angeles area where he works as an engineer. When he is not writing, he is a semi-professional stand-up comic, performing all over Southern California. Yvonne, his wife of 20 years, critiques everything and eggs him on to greater and greater silliness.

Y.B. Cats lives, writes, and edits in the American Southwest. yourblackcat.blogspot.com

LaVergne, TN USA
10 August 2010
192667LV00004B/70/P